Starseeker

The Valka Chronicles Book 2

S.A. McClure

Second Rule of the Coven...Survive at all costs

Starseeker

The Valka Chronicles Book 2

Written by S.A. McClure

Edited by Rainy Kaye
Cover Design by Jennifer Munswami of J.M. Rising Horse
Creations
https://www.facebook.com/groups/RysesCult/about/

Starseeker © August 2019 by S.A. McClure.
All Rights Reserved.
ISBN: 978-0-9992642-7-0

Lunameed Publishing
lunameed@gmail.com
Indianapolis, Indiana

This is a work of fiction. Names, places, characters and incidents are either the product of the author's imagination or are used fictitiously, and any resemblance to any actual persons, living or dead, organizations, events or locales is entirely coincidental.

Chapter One

Iris

"Iris."

The wind carried the whisper of her name, drawing her from her thoughts. The sound of his voice sent a shiver of warmth down her spine. She whirled around, searching the woods for Liam, dreading that it had just been a figment of her imagination.

Silver-blue eyes gleamed from the shadows. Leaves rustled as his form separated from the darkness and into glittering moonlight. His skin undulated with currents of lightning as he stared at her. His form flickered like dying candlelight. Iris stretched out a hand to take his, but her fingers passed through him.

"Find me."

His tone was plaintive. There was a hint of pain there that tore at her heart.

It had been months since he'd chosen to follow Grandmother. Months since she'd heard his voice. Months since she'd held him.

But he wasn't really there.

He was just an apparition of the man she loved. Night after night, she waited for him. She willed him to return to the place they'd first met, once upon a dream. He never had.

Until now.

"Find me," he whispered again.

His outline glittered like midnight onyx. The edges of him began to disappear.

"Where are you?" she cried. Claws grappled with her heart, squeezing the breath from her. She longed to touch his face, to feel the warmth of his hand in hers. "Tell me where to find you," she whispered into the night.

He smiled at her, his features flickering as if he were struggling to stay in the dreamworld.

"You promised you'd always find me," he said.

She shook her head. "That was a long time ago, Liam. I waited for you for months. I begged the Creators to let me see you again." Her voice trembled as she spoke, and she could barely hear her thoughts over the pounding of her heart. "You never came."

She peered into his eyes. He'd betrayed her. Broken her. Left her to die. In her loneliest moments, she hated him. But now, as he met her gaze, she couldn't force herself to let go of the love she felt for him. It was a deep-seated pit in the bottom of her heart. Hard. Unyielding. Stuck.

She shook her head.

A voice whispered in the recesses of her mind. He hadn't even glanced at her when he'd left with Grandmother Rel. She'd nearly died from the banshee's attack and he just' left her there to die.

"I don't have much time," Liam murmured. His voice was like velvet.

2

His face faded into the shadows. She reached out to him, willing him to stay just a little bit longer. There was a shimmer to the air as the outline of his face reemerged.

He jolted, as if being struck from behind. His eyes rolled to the back of his head before he slumped forward. And then, he was gone, as if he had never been there at all.

She swiped her hands through the space he'd just been occupying. She knew it was futile.

Sighing, she followed the thread she'd left for herself back to the real world. Her eyes fluttered open as she woke from her dream.

She leapt from her bed and stretched. With her nights spent prowling the dreamworld and her days spent training with her sister, she had barely any time to think about Liam.

At least, that's the lie she told herself. She still thought about him every moment of every day. A part of her knew he would always be a part of her life. It didn't matter how many times he left her or let her down. She was drawn to him. He was like the drug she needed to keep surviving.

And now, he was asking for her help.

She threw on her tunic draped over the chair in the corner, never mind that it was crusted in sweat from her previous swordplay with Micah. She pulled on a pair of leather pants she found wadded in the bottom of her closet, and then pulled open her door and rushed down the corridor.

When she and her comrades had first arrived at the manor house, it had been a run-down, boarded up mess. It'd taken a week just to clean the main floor enough to be habitable by the fifteen of them. Since then, they'd expanded into the east and west wings along with the second floor. She wasn't sure how the house had been overlooked for as long as it apparently had been. Although it was hidden between mountain peaks and surrounded by forest, she would have thought that someone would have known about it. Despite its dilapidated appearance, hints of grandeur gleamed through the dust and grime. She could envision its history.

Micah was exactly where she'd anticipated. The manor gardens had been overrun by wild flowers and weeds when they'd arrived. He had spent hours in the garden, pruning, weeding, and replanting. They'd found seeds stockpiled in one of the storage rooms along with gloves and other gardening tools. It was too soon to tell if the little seedlings would survive what remained of the colder spring months, though. Dramadoon was known for its bitterly cold and lengthy winters. He contended that doing the work was the first step. What came next was to believe in the future they hoped to build.

She was, however, taken aback at finding her sister in the garden with him. That was one of the things that had changed for the better since they'd left Balkeen's lair. Although Emma still hadn't recovered all her memories from the days they'd spent fighting for their lives against the monsters the Silver Skull coven had sent to kill them, she'd started to trust Micah. Iris knew he loved Emma more than anything. Time and time again, he'd fought to save her. It was ignorance that drove her sister to distrust him. A half-smile crested her lips as she regarded them together. Emma had even invited him to go hunting with her a few times. It wasn't much, but it was progress.

A loud snicking cut through the air as Micah snapped a pair of sheers shut. Emma sat on a bench, sharpening a set of daggers. Sparks flew from the blade as she ground the stone against it.

"What's wrong?" Micah didn't look up from the bush he was pruning as he spoke.

"What makes you think there's something wrong?" Iris asked as she picked up one of Emma's daggers. She ran her thumb over its edge. Blood dotted her skin and she hissed as she dropped the blade to the ground.

"For starters, you never come out here unless there's something wrong," Micah said, oblivious to the fact that she'd just cut herself.

Iris shared a look with her sister, who just shrugged as if to say, 'he's right, you know.'

Iris rolled her eyes.

"I saw Liam tonight," she said.

Micah snapped the pruners shut and cleared his throat. He peeked around the bush. Dirt was smeared across his forehead and there were damp splotches on his shirt. Lines creased his face. Iris knew they mirrored the lines on her own.

He leaned against the tree, crossing his arms over his chest. The muscles in his jaw clenched and unclenched as he waited for her to say more.

She glanced at her sister. Emma stared back at her, face pale. Only she had witnessed the nights Iris had spent restless, searching for Liam in the dreamworld. Only she knew how desperately Iris wanted to believe there had been some other explanation for why he'd chosen Grandmother over her. She hadn't been their real grandmother, just a witch who had raised them, lied to them, and then left them both for dead. Gooseflesh coated Iris's flesh. She wrapped her arms around her body and shivered.

"He asked me to find him." She chewed on her bottom lip as she considered her next words carefully. "There was something wrong with him. He kept flickering, as if there was something— or someone—stopping him from fully entering the dreamworld. He asked me to save him."

She looked between her sister and Micah, silently begging them to understand her need. She could see in Micah's expression that he knew what she was about to ask.

"You have to try," he said.

She turned her whole body around so that she was facing her sister.

"There's no other option," Emma continued. "You love him. He's lost, but he wants to be found." She shrugged. "Honestly, Iris, that's all you really have to know. You don't need our permission to go."

For the first time in months, Iris felt the tension begin to melt away from her shoulders. She hadn't wanted to admit it, especially to herself, but from the moment Liam had left with Grandmother, she'd wanted to seek him out. She'd wanted to find him. To let him know that he could still come back to her when he was ready.

She'd forced herself to stay busy with the day-to-day tasks of setting up their new home. She'd pushed herself to become a leader within their small family. And she'd risen up.

But she couldn't let his cry for help go unanswered. She couldn't abandon him, even though she had the terrible fear that he would break her heart even further.

"This is the closest contact with him since he vanished with Myrella," Micah said. "This could be your only chance to find him."

She met Micah's gaze. They had been friends—him and Liam. She should have known that he would want her to find him.

He frowned at his hands, his lips puckered into a disenchanted expression. "But I don't think you should go alone."

"Nor do I," Emma chimed in. "Which is why I'm going with you."

Iris opened her mouth to protest, but Emma simply laid her fingers over her lips, stilling the questions bubbling there.

"No," she said, "I don't want to hear any complaining from you. I'm going with you and that's final."

Iris sighed. Her sister was as stubborn as a mule on a hot summer day.

"Fine. But if you get in my way—even for just a moment—know that I'll leave you behind." The moment she said it, she knew it wasn't true. She could never abandon her sister. She was just frustrated that at the situation in which they found themselves. She wanted to protect the humans she'd freed from their curses. She wanted to grow her abilities. She wanted to give Emma time to fully recover from her near-death experience. But those things conflicted with her need to find Liam.

Micah leaned forward and placed his hand on Iris's shoulder. He held her gaze for a moment. There was so much understanding and acceptance in his expression.

"We won't give you a reason to leave us behind," he said.

Iris nodded. It still felt strange having someone share her burdens who wasn't Emma. Her throat bobbed as he bowed his head at her.

Emma set aside her tools and rose from the bench. She stepped forward and wrapped her arm around Iris's middle. She hugged her tight and pressed her brow against Iris's.

"I don't know when, I don't know how, but I can promise you this: we will find him," she said.

"Even if it takes us a lifetime to do so," Micah agreed.

Iris stood in silence with them, wrapped in the warmth of her friend and her sister. She knew it was unlikely that they would return without new scars to add to their already twisted souls and bodies. Liam and Micah had been friends for centuries and Emma would do anything to make her happy.

All the fires they'd been through had forged them into warriors. As long as they remained together, they could face down any obstacle. They could save Liam.

She drew them in close to her. Inhaled in their scents. Felt the warm, damp air of their breath puff against her skin. She smiled. They were a family.

Emma pulled away from her side. Her face was flushed and there was silver in her pupils. Her eyes glazed over and she seemed to peer beyond Iris altogether. She swayed.

"What is it?" Iris asked, reaching for her. "What's wrong?"

Emma's jaw tightened. She stared straight ahead. Her long, auburn hair fluttered in the wind that swept by them with the promise of spring.

Micah cupped Emma's cheeks, caressing her skin with his thumb.

He bent towards her, until their noses were nearly touching. "Emma?"

Still, Emma did not respond.

Iris shared a worried glance with Micah. Her heart thudded in her chest as she gripped Emma's hand and squeezed.

Emma did not return the gesture.

Iris opened her mouth to speak.

Emma began to glow a brilliant cobalt blue. She stretched out a single hand. Her entire body quivered as she pointed towards the northern star. Tiny rivers of blue light coursed over her skin, as if it were flowing through her veins. Iris traced the lines with the tip of her fingertip, barely grazing her sister's skin.

Emma stood motionless, her eyes fixed on a spot towards the heavens.

"We should take her to the infirmary."

The rough sound of Micah's voice broke Iris out of her reverie.

"Yes," she said. "We should."

They prodded Emma gently towards the door. She didn't struggle against them, but she didn't walk on her own accord either. Sweat coated her brow and upper lip and stained her undergarments yellow. Although Emma continued to point towards the northern star, she allowed them to guide her into the manor.

Iris peered into the shadowy corridors. She must have walked these halls hundreds of times over the months they'd been here. The sound of trickling water and the scent of mold greeted them. Iris couldn't say she enjoyed the smell, but she had certainly gotten used to it.

The door slammed shut behind them.

Emma screamed.

"What's wrong with her?" Iris asked, her voice cracking.

Micah grunted in response. He clamped his hand over Emma's mouth, but she jabbed him in the gut before stomping on his foot. She slammed her head into his nose. His jaw tightened and his eyes watered. Dropping his hold on her, he cupped his hand over his face.

Emma scrambled towards the door, the cobalt light flickering in her veins as she moved. She didn't look back as she swung the door open and raced into the trees.

"Emma! Wait!" Iris called.

She darted after her sister. She didn't see if Micah followed or if he'd gone for help. All she could think about reaching Emma.

When she finally caught up to her, she intertwined her fingers with her sister's and let her lead the way through the winding trees.

They abruptly stopped. Iris tottered on her toes.

Emma's face was placid, as if she had never experienced a single emotion in her life. She continued pointing at the northern star.

Iris gripped her sister's shoulders. Not even Emma's eyes fluttered as she continued to stare in the star's direction.

"Please, just tell me what's wrong."

She stroked a stray hair from Emma's cheeks. She couldn't lose her sister. She'd already sacrificed too much. Lost too much.

She snapped her fingers in front of Emma's face.

Emma didn't even look at her.

"Please, Emma."

She shook her. She begged her. She prayed to the Creators for guidance.

There was no response. Not from the Creators. Not from Emma. Not from anyone.

She brushed away the tears trailing down her own cheeks. They were pointless.

She cradled Emma close to her chest as she hummed a song they'd loved as children. It was a slow, melancholy tune, but it was the only thing she could think to do.

"Please," Iris whispered in her sister's ear. "Please, come back."

They stood, rooted in that spot with the trees bowing all around them. Icicles sparkled like diamonds, casting an array of color across the forest floor. It reminded Iris of the dreamworld where she'd met Liam.

Emma began to burn. Sweat soaked through her dress, dampening Iris's hands. She shook uncontrollably. Iris peered around the woods, searching for anything she could use to stop her sister's convulsions.

A burst of blue light exploded from Emma's chest, and a wave of power washed over her. She was thrown backwards, her head slamming into a tree. She crumpled to the forest floor. It was all she could do to keep her eyes open and fixed on Emma.

The cobalt light coursing through Emma's veins streamed from her outstretched finger, forming a brilliant line that disappeared into the darkness. Iris squinted, trying to determine how far it stretched, but could see no end to its light.

"I don't know when. I don't know how."

Emma's raspy voice caught her off guard. Iris ran to her sister's side and crouched beside her.

She touched Emma's shoulder. "You don't know what?"

Emma passed her hand through the light still streaming from her fingertips. "It's him, Iris. It's Liam."

"I don't—"

"I can't explain it."

She clasped Iris's hand, stilling it. "What are you saying?"

Her heart thundered in her chest.

"Isn't it obvious?" Emma squeezed her hand. "I can feel him, Iris. I can't explain it, but I know that if we follow this path, it'll lead us straight to him."

Iris sank to her knees and wrapped her arms around Emma. They sat in silence for a moment. Iris squinted into the distance. For a moment, she could imagine that Liam could see the light too. She could believe that he knew they were coming for him. That she would save him.

Leaning back, she peered into her sister's eyes and smiled. Heat coursed through her veins as she as she whispered, "I guess you're a witch, too."

"I guess I am."

Chapter Two
Emma

Find him.

No matter how long it took or what the cost was, she needed to find Liam. Her sister's happiness meant everything to her and finding him was the only way of seeing her smile.

Mud and leaves stuck to her boots as she squelched through the forest. Drizzling rain chilled her, creating gooseflesh on her arms. It had been like this for over three days now without reprieve. Even her water-resistant cloak was heavy and damp.

Although she didn't fully understand her powers, she knew she was the only one who could find him. Whenever she focused on him, her veins coursed with blue light and she could somehow sense what path to follow to find him. It was like lightning coursing through her body. Each step she took pulsed with energy. It drove her to follow the thin line of blue light that

S.A. McClure

exploded from her chest each time her abilities engaged. So far, she'd only been able to maintain the tracking ability for a few minutes before it snuffed out entirely. Thankfully, she knew the forest well enough to guide them through it.

She had spent her childhood exploring these forests and hunting what little there was to eat. There was even less now. Her stomach rumbled and cramped. Gritting her teeth, she continued to trudge forward.

She had nearly died in that ravine. Bones broken, her precious lifeblood seeping from her. She had blacked out for most of it, but there were moments when she slept when a chill seeped into her bones and she felt the complete numbness that came with death.

A branch snapped, and she held up her fist, stilling Micah and Iris as they trailed behind her. Silently, she slipped a dagger from her belt and crouched low to the ground. It was a practiced move that she'd used multiple times before during her hunt for food.

Her ears prickled as the sound of more twigs snapping. She sniffed at the air. Nothing smelled amiss. Dropping to her knees, she crawled forward, towards the sound of cracking branches. Whatever had joined them in the forest was large. Larger than any animal had a right to be.

Ducking below a low hanging branch, she emerged into a clearing. Tall grass grew in the center of the circle, waving in a gentle breeze. Not a single animal made a sound. Her muscles tensed and her breathing slowed. The air was dense in this place. Starbugs flitted around the edges of the clearing, but they didn't move into it. She held up her hand to stop her sister from entering the space.

Too late.

Iris stepped into the edge middle of the field. The air undulated as if it were a soap bubble about to pop. Emma rushed forward, reaching out to take her sister's hand. Her footfalls slowed. Her mind still worked, but her body froze to the spot where both feet landed in the field. She couldn't feel anything. Her eyes flicked to Micah as he hung back on the perimeter of the clearing.

His frown told her everything. He wasn't going to save them.

She should have known. After all this time, he was still just a cowardly Szarmian. How long had he been biding his time until the right moment to just let them die?

Iris's skin began to glitter. It was as if thousands of stars had suddenly kindled to life. Her lips parted but no sound came. She closed her eyes, her brow furrowing into deep lines.

Fissures erupted along the air. Emma's eyes widened as feeling flooded back into her legs. She lifted her foot ever so slightly.

Iris shook violently. Her teeth chattered as the light clinging to her skin began to lift off her in particles of sparkling dust. Her already pale skin turned ashen as her feet rose from the ground.

"Iris!" Micah screamed as he lassoed her with a vine. It disintegrated into dust the moment it touched her skin.

The invisible manacles holding Emma in place released their hold on her entirely. Her legs gave out, and she fell to one knee. Sweat dripped from her brow as she stared up at her sister.

Micah threw another vine to Emma. She wound it around her stomach as he pulled her to him. He crouched beside her and cupped her cheeks in his hands. His dark eyes roamed over her face, concern etched in every line and crease. She gritted her teeth against the kindness in his eyes. Her heart fluttered slightly as his thumb caressed her skin. Not today. Maybe not ever.

She supposed she would have to forgive him for the thoughts she'd had only moments ago about him abandoning them. At every turn he proved her wrong. It was infuriating.

Thunder cracks without lightning shook the world around them. Emma turned her gaze to her sister's floating body. Wrenching her face free from Micah's hold, she scrambled to her feet. She shielded her eyes against her sister's brilliance.

"Come on, Iris," she whispered.

Iris's body shuddered.

Micah stood beside Emma. He slipped his hand into hers as they stared up at the floating body above them. Streaks of purple tinged in black coursed over Iris's veins, as if she were absorbing poison. Emma clung to his hand. It was the only thing grounding her. She wanted nothing more than to rush in and yank her sister from the heavens. To save her. Just as she always had.

But there was no way of reaching her.

The air all around the clearing turned opaque. It hardened into a crystalline structure with fissures racing across its surface. Emma placed a hand against the hard line of air. It was warm to the touch, almost feverish. She jerked her hand back as the spot she'd just tapped dissolved.

Trusting her instincts, she began running her hands over the opaque wall of air. Every place her skin touched puffed into dust. Without being asked, Micah followed her lead. Together, the destroyed the lower half of the wall and started on the top.

Iris gasped loudly. She fell from the sky at an alarming rate as the rest of the barrier shuddered and vanished, as if it had never existed.

Emma rushed forward to catch her sister. She wasn't going to make it in time. Despite her training, she wasn't fast enough. She lunged forward, tripping on a log hidden in the tall grass.

Micah grunted as he caught Iris in his arms. Emma hadn't even seen him rushing forward. His shoulders shuddered under her sudden weight, but he didn't drop her to the ground. Instead, he cradled her to his chest and, straightening, strode from the clearing. gently laid her onto a bed of moss beside a tree. Emma hurried to join him.

Iris's cheeks were so pale, they were nearly translucent. Emma placed a trembling hand on her brow. She was burning up. She snatched her hand back and leaned in close.

"You have to tell me which herbs will help you," she whispered. "You're the potion-maker of the two of us."

Iris didn't stir. Not a blink. Or a whoosh of air as she breathed in.

"Iris?" she asked, fear creeping into her. She shook her sister's shoulders.

Iris's head lopped from side-to-side.

"Please be okay," Emma whispered.

14

She pressed her ear to Iris's breast and listened. She couldn't hear a heartbeat.

She pounded her fist in Iris's chest. She wasn't exactly sure what she was doing, but she'd seen Grandmother Rel perform a similar procedure when a mountaineer fell from a tree and broke his back. He, too, didn't have a heartbeat when he'd first arrived at the cottage. She pumped her fist into her chest over and over again until her knuckles turned red.

Micah gripped her shoulders. "Let her go," he whispered from behind her. "You can't save her now."

Emma glared up at him.

"You know nothing of what it means to be a family." She growled as she redoubled her efforts. "Breathe!" she screamed, and then pressed her lips against Iris's and forced her breath into her sister's lungs.

Iris's chest rose and fell as the air expanded her lungs and then left again.

"I am not giving up on you!" Emma whispered. "Do you hear me?"

Her arms shook and her wrists ached from pounding on Iris's chest. Micah didn't try to stop her again.

Just when she didn't know if she could pump her sister's chest another time, Iris sputtered and then coughed. Her eyes were glassy when she opened them, and she grimaced at the bright light from the sun.

Emma wrapped her arms around Iris's shoulders and pulled her up into a tight embrace. Tears streamed down her cheeks as she sobbed into her sister's hair.

"I thought I'd lost you," she whispered.

Iris tightened her grip around Emma's shoulders. "I will always find my way back to you." She laughed. "And, even if I didn't, I have no doubt that you'd use this newfound tracking skill of yours to hunt me down."

They both laughed. Emma felt as if she were watching the scene from outside her body. She was numb and yet overwhelmingly relieved at the same time.

"What happened?" she asked.

Iris shrugged. "The clearing was cursed. I get the sense it was one of the coven witches."

Emma's jaw fell open. The coven had sent a bevy of creatures to kill them only a few short months ago. They'd even enlisted Micah and Liam to attempt to kill them, but somehow, they'd fought against their orders and helped save them instead. At least Micah had. She still wasn't sure about Liam's role in all of this. One minute he was saving their lives, the next he was betraying them. He'd left with the hag who'd raised them, Grandmother Rel, the moment Iris freed him from his curse. If Iris hadn't been so committed to saving him, she would have left him to suffer the consequences of his betrayal.

She knew they'd been bent on killing Iris because of her ability to break spells, but she hadn't realized they'd resorted to setting traps for them.

She jerked her head back to Iris.

"Have you been wandering the dreamworld again?" she asked, harshly. Iris knew every time she entered that place to search for Liam she put her safety at risk. The coven had been able to trap her there once—had nearly killed her in the process.

Iris didn't meet her gaze as she whispered, "Yes."

"You know how dangerous it is!" Emma shouted. She sprang to her feet and stepped away from her sister. "I'm tracking him, remember? You don't have to put yourself—or me, I might add—at risk by wandering in that place!" Doubt clenched her abdomen like a bear's claws. She wasn't in complete control of her tracking ability yet. Still, that didn't matter. Her jaw ached as she clenched her teeth together and glared at her sister.

"I know," Iris replied timidly. "Believe me, I know the risks. I think about them every time I search for his dreams." She wrung her hands in her lap. Her lower lip extended slightly. "But I yearn to hear his voice again, Emma. Just once I want to know he's okay."

Micah stepped between them. "We don't have time for this," he chided. He peered down at Iris. "If what you say is true and the coven set this as a trap, then we need to leave this place. Now."

He lifted Iris to her feet and gave Emma a pointed look that seemed to say, 'no more arguing.' Emma fought the urge to stick her tongue out at him. She didn't care if that made her childish or not. Her sister needed to learn how to start assessing the risks of her decisions before she got everyone around her killed. Including them.

Emma led the way through the trees, Micah beside her. Iris trailed behind them.

Emma's stomach growled slightly. She needed to eat if she was going to be strong enough to use her tracking ability again. She still didn't fully understand how she was able to sense him. He was basically a stranger to her. She'd barely shared more than a dozen words with him.

But Iris loved him.

And, she supposed, that was enough for her to give up renovating the manor house to travel north to rescue the poor soul.

Iris stumbled and fell farther behind.

"Do we need to slow down?" Emma asked, barely glancing over her shoulder.

Iris still had not regained her color following the trap. Her cheeks appeared more sunken and her hair clung to her face.

"No," she replied breathily. "I'm fine. I just need to. Catch. My. Breath."

Her words came out stilted.

"Are you sure about that?" Emma asked.

"Of course," she said as her breathing slowly returned to normal. She swayed slightly.

"Alright, that's enough," Emma said, slowing to match her sister's pace. She wrapped her arm around Iris's waist and supported her as they moved forward. "You clearly need rest."

"No, I can keep going," Iris said. "Please, Emma. He's out there. All alone."

"Not quite," Emma said, callously. "Or did you forget that he's with Grandmother Rel?"

Iris glared at her. "And that makes it better, how?" She huffed. "The more time we waste, the longer she has to dig her claws deeper into him. She could be hurting him, Emma. I haven't seen him since he asked me to find him. It's been over a week now!" Her cheeks reddened as she spoke and she chewed on her bottom lip. "I know he's out there. I know she's doing terrible things to him. I know you can't summon your ability on command all the time yet. I get it. Trust me. I do. But..." she trailed off. "If I have to push myself past exhaustion to find him, I will. Please try to understand, Emma."

Emma caught her sister's hand in her own and squeezed. "Listen to me. Whether we find him tomorrow or several years from now, I promise you that as long as you think he's breathing, we'll keep searching."

Iris wobbled.

"Can you carry her?" Emma asked without looking at Micah.

She already knew the answer would be yes. So far, he had agreed to nearly everything she asked of him. Not that she asked much. Iris told her that he had been a faithful companion to her and, in her dreams, she sometimes remembered his kind eyes. But that didn't mean that she could trust him.

In response, he scooped Iris into his arms.

"Thank you," Emma said.

She sighed heavily and focused on Liam. Although she had never actually seen his face in person, Iris had described him enough that she somehow felt like she knew all the details of his features. Although she could sense him without imagining a face, it helped cement what she was searching for in her mind.

A thin, wavering blue light shot from her chest and weaved between the trees. She motioned for the other two to trail her and began following the light's path.

The wind picked up the farther they walked. The earthy scent of rain filled the air before the first drop of water fell on her head. Summers in the Beoscuret Mountains were never warm, but unlike the dead of winter when everything was blanketed in snow, summer meant torrential downpours.

"We need to find shelter," she shouted just as a flash of lightning cleaved the sky in two.

Iris jolted and buried her face into Micah's shoulder.

He set Iris on the ground and withdrew a map from his satchel. Although rain poured all around them, their clothes, packs, and the map remained dry. One of the cursed humans they'd saved from Balkeen's lair was an enchantress who specialized in protection spells. Rain repellent spells were, apparently, quite popular when she worked for the crown. But that was before she'd been kidnapped by Balkeen and turned into a fox.

Before they'd left the manor house, she'd enchanted everything they wanted to keep dry. Until now, they hadn't had a chance to test the enchantments' effectiveness.

"We're close to a village." He pointed slightly to the right of where the blue light led. "If we go this way, we'll reach it within the hour."

Iris frowned. "That's out of our way."

"Yes, but we've been on the road for several days now and you just almost died. I'm sorry, Iris, but I think we're going to have to out vote you on this one."

Emma lifted her chin and narrowed her eyes as Iris looked between her and Micah. To his credit, Micah remained stoic, even when Iris's lip began to tremble.

"Fine," she said with a hiss. "But, just so you know, the longer it takes for us to find him, the more likely it is that I'll venture out on my own."

Emma rolled her eyes. "You wouldn't last out here. You don't even know how to light a fire without a starter."

"Well," Iris began. She stopped, her eyes growing wider as she fought to find the perfect comeback.

Emma smirked at her. "It's okay, Iris. You can make potions and heal people like you're a Creator. All I can do is hunt and survive."

Iris smiled. "Together we make an unbeatable pair."

"We do."

"Alrighty then, if you're done building each other up, I would like to get out of this rain before the enchantment wears off," Micah said as he bent to pick Iris up again.

"I can walk," she said, slipping away from him.

They marched on in silence towards the town. Emma extinguished the blue light emanating from her chest and squeezed in between Iris and Micah.

She wrapped her arm around her sister's waist and leaned in to whisper, "When can we ditch him again?" She jerked her thumb towards Micah. "He's kind of a drag."

Iris smirked. "I believe, dear sister, that we must bring him with us. Two young, unchaperoned women will draw attention. At least if he's around, we have a cover."

Although Emma knew her sister was right, she hated admitting it. She stole a glance at Micah. He caught her eye and smiled. She shrugged and turned back to Iris.

"Fine," she mumbled. "But if we ever get the chance to get rid—"

"You know I can hear you, right?" Micah interrupted, his voice husky and deep.

Emma whirled on him, her cheeks already flushing.

"I'm literally walking right beside you. I know you have the power to track people, but you certainly don't have the ability to be quiet," he said.

She cocked an eyebrow at him, surprised that he was speaking that brusquely to her. Even when she'd been rude to him before, he'd always been polite to her. She crossed her arms over her chest and scowled at him.

He shoved past her. She grasped him arm to halt him, and his nostrils flared.

"Look, I'm not trying to be rude or mean to you," she said. "But we barely know you—"

He ripped his arm free from her grasp, turning to her. "You know, for someone who is supposed to be fearless, passionate, and brave, you seem to have a hard time understanding even the most basic of emotions," he said. "I've tried everything to get you to remember me and still you refuse to open your mind and heart to the possibility that all I want is to be by your side."

Emma's heart thudded loudly in her ears. Part of her wanted to trust him. To let him comfort her. To let him be her person. But every time he began to chip away at her barriers, she remembered what Grandmother Rel had done to them. She'd let the cockatrice stalk, hunt, and kill her. She'd left Iris for dead. So, although she wanted to let him in, panic hovered over her at the thought of letting her guard down. She was the huntress. She needed to keep her guard up at all costs. Even if left fissures racing across her heart.

She breathed in deeply, readying a snarky response when, from the corner of her eye, she saw Iris slink ahead of them. She gritted her teeth. She would have to have a discussion with her later about abandoning her in her time of need. Of course, Iris had been pushing her and Micah together since the day they fought against the cockatrice. Not that she remembered the battle much.

Micah placed a warm hand on her shoulder and squeezed. "I know it's been difficult for you. I understand that you've been through so much in such a short amount of time. But do you have any idea how it feels to have you constantly goad me? To push me aside like I am nothing more than a pebble in your shoe?"

She opened her mouth to respond, but he leaned down and kissed her before she could speak.

His lips were warm and only the tiniest bit chapped as he leaned into her. The kiss lasted for a fleeting moment, but it left her feeling lightheaded.

He pulled back. His eyes were slit as he looked down at her. They trained on her lips.

His touch lingered on her like a phantom. A warm, making-her-toes-curl phantom.

She stepped back, creating some space between them.

"What was that for?" she asked. She looked down at her feet as she spoke, not willing to meet his gaze.

"That was me trying to convince you that all those subtle feelings you have for me are real. Just because you don't consciously remember me, doesn't mean that a piece of what we have isn't locked away somewhere inside you. We were friends, Emma." He reached up and stroked her hair. "I want us to always be friends."

"Umm, Emma," Iris said, and Emma jumped.

She turned to face her sister. "What is it?"

Her heart hammered wildly in her chest.

Iris pointed towards the village. A group of men strode down the street. Although they bore no uniforms, Emma suspected they were military men. She sucked in a deep breath. This wasn't part of the plan.

Although relations between Szarmi and Dramadoon were better than they ever had been before, there was still a lot of resentment towards Szarmians. With Micah's dark skin and brown eyes, it would be obvious he was a Szarmian and Emma didn't want to draw attention to their movements. It was bad enough having the Silver Skull coven tracking them. She didn't want a mob of ignorant, angry farmers chasing them down.

"What are we going to do?" Iris asked, stepping behind a tree until only the smallest portion of her face was visible beyond the forest line.

"I'm not sure," Emma said.

"We go down there, book a room in the inn, and pretend like nothing is amiss," Micah said. He didn't look at Emma as he observed the village.

Iris motioned towards the guards. "We can't go in there now!"

"Yes, we can," he said, "and we will."

He stepped forward until the torchlight on the guard tower lit up his face. Emma hesitated before linking arms with Iris and pulling her forward with her.

Iris stumbled a bit and Emma could see the exhaustion etched in the planes of her face. She needed rest in a proper bed. And this was how they were going to achieve that.

Micah ushered them forward. Although he didn't say anything, his tension was obvious in the tautness of his shoulders. He lugged all three of their packs without complaint as they crossed a circle of white stone and entered the village.

Someone grabbed Emma's arm.

"What are you doing here?" a male snapped as he threw her to the ground.

Chapter Three

Emma

A rock sliced Emma's cheek when she fell. She moaned softly as she touched the place where blood was freely flowing from her flesh.

"What are you doing!" Micah roared as he charged towards the man who'd thrown her to the ground. The man drew his sword and pointed it at Micah.

"Seems to me you best be polite to us," the man said. "My friends and I were paid to protect this village from bandits and thieves. State your business, or we'll cut you down like the swine you are."

"Do we look like bandits and thieves to you?" Emma asked, struggling to sit. She ripped a length of cloth from her undershirt and pressed it to her cheek. The cut stung, but nothing worth crying over.

The man looked them over and grunted. "I suppose not, but one can never be too careful."

"I promise you, we're just weary travelers looking for shelter for the night." Emma bowed her head to him as she spoke.

The man pause. His sword still jutted out from his hand, pointed directly at her. Emma resisted the urge to fidget as she waited for him to respond. After another few seconds, he sighed heavily and lowered his arm.

"Tavern and inn is just a few paces down the way," he said as he jerked his thumb behind his head. "Ask for Mrs. Sanders. She'll get you set right straight."

"Thank you," Iris murmured as she stepped out from behind the tree. She headed down the path.

Emma pushed to her feet and rushed to catch up to her sister. Iris wobbled with each step she took. Emma caught her just before she collapsed to the ground. She sank to her knees, easing Iris down until she was laying flat on the road.

"Eh, what's wrong with her?" the man asked, coming up behind them. "If she's sick, we don't want none of that here. We heard 'bout the plague killin' people in the town to the north."

Emma fumbled over her words, unsure how to assure the man that her sister didn't have the plague. She briefly thought about telling him the truth, but she doubted saying that her sister was on the kill list of a powerful coven of witches would do much to ease his concerns.

To her surprise, Micah stepped forward and place a hand on the man's shoulder. "She is just tired from the journey. We came from the south, anyway."

Iris moaned softly as Emma clutched her closer to her chest. The man stared down at her blankly.

"You're sure she doesn't have it?" he asked. His eyes lingered on Iris's pale cheeks and sweaty brow. "Maybe the doc should check her out before—"

"That won't be necessary," Micah replied calmly. "We will have a healer meet with her once she's rested a bit from the journey." He pulled a silver star from his breast pocket and placed it in the man's hand. "We mean you no trouble and we will be gone by first light."

Although the man still stared warily at Iris, he clasped the coin in his hand.

"Bah," he finally said, "I suppose if you'll be gone the mornin' there ain't much harm in you being here for the night."

Emma sighed in relief. She mouthed a quick 'thank you' to Micah before aiding Iris to her feet. She ushered her down the road, Micah right behind.

The streets were eerily silent as they walked down them. Emma wondered what had caused the heightened security. It seemed strange to her that no one would be in the streets at this time of night.

They passed by a house with a second story. A child sat at the window, his candle flickering in the dark night. Emma caught his gaze as they walked by. His eyes bulged and he quickly drew the shutters shut on the windows.

"Do you get the feeling that something is amiss here?" Iris muttered under her breath. "This place seems off."

Emma tugged her closer to her, her eyes flicking from side-to-side as she tried to determine what, if any, threats lurked in the shadows. The town did seem strange, but they were here now and Iris's condition had only worsened the longer they'd traveled. She needed rest and relaxation if she was going to continue their journey.

"Micah," Iris said hoarsely, "what do you think of this place?"

He didn't say anything, but Emma could see the caution in his eyes. Something about the town bothered him as well. She could only pray that whatever it was that was setting their teeth on edge would be much more benign than she was currently imagining.

Iris yawned, her jaw cracking.

"We'll be at the tavern soon," Emma whispered. She kissed Iris's cheek for good measure. She'd nearly lost her tonight. If there was anything she could do to show her sister just how much she meant to her, she wanted to do it. She needed to.

"This place echoes of pain and sorrow," Iris whispered. Her eyes glistened as she spoke.

"Well, that's not ominous and terrifying at all," Emma responded.

"Keep it moving," Micah said. Tension dripped from his every word.

"And you're certainly not helping with your stress-inducing tone," she grumbled at him.

He nudged her from behind. She bit back her retort. She hated how familiar he acted with her. She hated it even more that there was an element of ease in engaging with him, as if she already knew him.

When the inn sign came into view, she sighed in relief. They were minutes from a bed.

As they neared, she studied the sign. It depicted a dragon wrapped around its own body, devouring its own tail. She frowned. Something about it seemed vaguely familiar, but she couldn't place where she would have seen it before. She made a mental note to ask Iris about it later.

"Aeron's Tavern," she read.

"Come on," Micah said as he pushed past Emma and headed into the inn.

Emma followed without a word. The moment she crossed through the door, she felt like the air had been sucked from her lungs. It was oppressively hot inside. Despite the summer air, a roaring fire filled the hearth. Hardly anyone was in the tavern area. Only three tables were occupied: two by men dressed in similar attire as the guard who'd stopped them, and one by a lone travel. Whoever they were, they sat in the shadows.

Micah motioned towards Emma and Iris as he approached the innkeeper. He was a squat man with a jovial face. Or, at least, it would have been jovial except for the absolute terror in his eyes.

"We just need the room for a night," Micah whispered. "Please, my companion is in need of rest and a good meal."

The innkeeper's gaze darted towards Iris, his cheeks paling.

"I'm sorry, sir, but—" he started.

"But nothing," Emma cut in, stepping forward. "One of the guards told us to ask for a Mrs. Sanders. Said she'd get us set up for the night."

The innkeeper sputtered, his eyes growing wide.

"Are you sure he said to ask for her? Mrs. Sanders, that is?" he asked, his voice quivering.

"Yes," Emma replied, raising one eyebrow at him.

"One moment, please," he whispered, and then disappeared into one of the back rooms.

Emma tapped her foot as she waited for him to reappear. Micah gave her a reproachful look. She shook her head at him, annoyance filling her. His method didn't work. She didn't see any harm in doing what the guard had explicitly told them to do. Besides, now that they were here, the thought of a warm bed and hearty meal filled her with joy.

"Emma," Iris whispered. Her voice was so weak that Emma had to lean into her just to understand what she said. "We can't stay here. Please—"

"Nonsense." Emma shushed her. "We're here now. There's no reason to let anything stop you from wanting to enjoy this. I know you want to find Liam, but if you're not well enough to travel without stumbling and falling, then there's no point."

"You're right," Iris said, breathless. Her words were so labored.

"Shh," Emma said. "Save your energy until you're feeling stronger."

The innkeeper stepped around the corner just as an axe dug itself into the wood of the counter. Emma spun around to see three men, all brandishing weapons standing behind them. Micah dropped their packs to the ground and drew his sword. He took a defensive stance.

"I wouldn't do that if I were you," the innkeeper hissed from behind them.

"What's happening?" Iris murmured into Emma's ear. Her breath was hot and moist against her skin.

"Nothing," Emma whispered. She carefully knelt and laid Iris against the bar. At least she would be protected from behind in that position. She drew one of her daggers from her boot and swung it outward, menacingly.

"Tsk," the innkeeper said, "you think we're afraid of two weary travelers?"

"I thought you were going to help us," Emma replied. She pressed her back against Micah's and stared at the innkeeper. He smirked at her, his lips curling into an unpleasant smile.

"Mrs. Sanders doesn't want any more guests for the evening," he said as he trailed his fat fingers over his chin. "Of course, she could be persuaded if given the right amount of incentive."

"All this for a little coin?" Emma snapped.

The innkeeper shook his head. "No, of course not. You seem like just the type of folks who can fight when needed." He smiled at her in a way that made her skin crawl. "We are more than happy to provide aid to your little friend, as long as you do a favor for us. Consider it…payment for services rendered."

"Uh huh," Emma said, "And what, exactly, would these services be?"

"There's a monster plaguing our village. Kill the beast, and we'll heal your sister for you."

"How do we know we can trust you?" Micah asked. He brandished his sword outward as several men joined the three standing in the doorway. They filled in the space around them.

"Ah, yes, well that's the beauty of it all, isn't it?" The innkeeper smiled. "You can't."

Emma shared a look with Micah. She was ready to fight their way out of this mess. If her sister was to be believed, she'd fought a cockatrice and won. Sure, she'd lost her memories of the fight and she'd nearly died, but that didn't matter. She'd beaten the monster.

An idea occurred to her.

S.A. McClure

"If we fight this monster for you and win," she said, "you'll let us leave here unscathed. You'll heal my sister and provide us with supplies for our continued journey."

"But of course," the innkeeper replied smoothly. There was something about his tone that made Emma pause. She gripped her dagger more firmly in her hand, contemplating lodging it in the closest man's throat.

She envisioned the battle. With Micah fighting beside her, they could probably take out about half of their opponents. The other half would be a struggle and she wasn't confident they would be able to win against all of them. If they lost, she doubted they would show mercy to Iris. She refused to let her sister fall prey to them.

Huffing, she nodded.

"What are you doing?" Micah whispered so that only she could hear.

She nudged him with her elbow and whispered, "Later," before smiling broadly at the innkeeper. "So, what do we call you?"

The innkeeper bowed. "Mr. Damian Fooks at your service," he replied, "but you can call me Fooks."

He clapped his hands, and the men surrounding them lowered their weapons.

Emma desperately wanted to drop to her knees and cradle her sister. The sweat on her brow had increased and her eyes were glassy when they met hers. But she sensed that doing anything to comfort her sister would only bring them trouble.

"You'll leave at first light," Fooks said as he motioned towards his men. They left the room and returned seconds later carrying a large map. He laid it on the counter, and then stood guard next to the door.

Emma trailed her eyes over the map. Various places had been marked with a black skull with bleeding eyes. She recognized the area from the maps Grandmother Rel had kept in their cabin. She lingered on the spot where the dwarf, Balkeen, had kept his lair.

A deep ravine ran next to it where a river coursed through the mountain. That was the place she had almost died.

Fooks jabbed his finger at a spot on the map where there was a cluster of the skulls.

"This, here, is the place where the monster is currently residing," he said. "Bring me its head and I'll let you leave here unscathed, with your companion."

"And supplies," Emma reminded.

He blinked at her for a moment before adding, "With supplies."

Micah gripped her elbow in warning. With what she hoped was an inconspicuous motion, she pulled her arm out of his grip. She glanced down at Iris, who was now slumped fully on the floor with her eyes closed. Her chest rose and fell steadily, which was a good sign, but she didn't like how ashen her face was.

"What can you tell us about the monster?" she asked, dragging her eyes back to meet Fooks's gaze.

He shrugged. "It attacks at night. No one in my crew has actually seen it and survived." He swallowed hard and continued, "We've been tracking it on the princess's orders for months. Some of my best men are dead because of it."

She raised an eyebrow. "The princess ordered you to take a village hostage and force weary travelers to fight a monster for you?"

He chortled.

"She wants the job done," he replied vaguely.

It was all the answer Emma needed.

"Do you know how to kill it?" she asked.

"Rumor has it that it can only be killed by beheading and then burning the body. 'Course, you'll need to bring the head back to me so that I can prove to Princess Saphria that the job is done."

"Fine," Emma said. "Anything else you can tell us about it?"

"I heard it can take the form of anything it chooses," one of the men behind her said.

"It has great white fangs that its uses to drain your blood for a meal," another one whispered.

S.A. McClure

"It is mist and shadow," said another.

"You make it seem like this beast is unbeatable," she whispered. She resisted the urge to peer down at her sister's face.

"Whether it is or isn't has no bearing on our deal," Fooks said, casting a stern eye on his men. "You agreed to fight it. If you die, I promise I'll give yer sister to one of the women in the town to care for her until she's well enough to leave on her own."

Emma bared her teeth. Leaving Iris here put her in danger. The coven could cast another curse. They could find her while she was in this weakened state. If both she and Micah left her unattended, there would be no one here to protect her.

"You have to let me go alone," Emma whispered, meeting Micah's gaze.

He glared at her and shook his head.

"You have to," she plead "We can't leave Iris—"

"Leave the lass with me," a female voice boomed from behind them.

Emma turned to face a tall woman with tattoos coursing over her skin. Her dark hair was a mixture of braids and wild curls that left Emma with the impression that the woman could have been raised by wolves.

"Who are you?" Micah asked gruffly, stepping in front of Emma.

The woman cast him a sly smile as she looked beyond him to meet Emma's gaze.

"I promise I won't let any harm come to her," she said.

Emma didn't know why, but she trusted this woman. She'd never met her before. She didn't have any reason to believe that she would protect Iris. But she certainly didn't have any faith in the men holding them hostage. She didn't doubt that, if left to their own devices, they would either physically or emotionally harm her sister. At best, they would simply neglect her until whatever side effects she was experiencing from breaking the spell wore off.

"Why should we believe you?" Micah barked at the woman.

She turned a steely gaze towards him. "Because I am the only person here who is willing to provide aid to your companion in your absence. I would suggest that you show a little more respect."

Emma held up her hands in a placating way. She jerked her head towards Micah who leaned in close so that they could whisper to one another without being heard.

"What choice do we have?" Emma asked.

He slit his eyes and stared at her. She'd never seen him look so angry in their entire six months together.

"I should stay," he said. "That's what you wanted. To go face the beast on your own." He lifted his hand as if he were going to touch her cheek. Sorrow filled his eyes and he balled his hand into a fist.

She blinked at him, surprised.

"We have an alternative," she said.

"What? Leaving your sister in the hands of a complete stranger? No. That is not an alternative, Emma. What if she's part of the coven? What if she was sent here and has orchestrated this whole debacle?"

She hadn't considered that. It was possible. The woman was of the right age. And very beautiful. Emma wouldn't have been surprised if she were part of a coven, even if she weren't a member of the one trying to murder them.

"It's a risk we have to take, Micah. They won't let us leave here with Iris if we don't fight the monster and we are too outnumbered to have a chance at fighting our way out. Especially with Iris in her current condition."

He huffed. Resignation set his jaw firmly in place as he nodded once at her.

"Then it's settled," she said, a smile touching her lips.

"Yes."

She reached out and squeezed his hand. He looked at her, surprise etched over his face. She smiled before pulling away from him.

"Fine," she said, turning to the woman, "but I want to break bread with you first."

The woman nodded. "But of course."

Emma ordered two bowls of the tavern stew and a pint of cider each for her and Micah before wandering over the woman's table. Micah carried Iris to the table and laid her on the bench to continue resting. Her chest rose and fell steadily, but she didn't open her eyes.

Emma surveyed the tavern, then laughed as she realized this woman had been in the room the entire time. She'd been the lone traveler tucked away in the shadows when they first arrived.

"My name is Chiara," the woman said, taking a seat across from Emma, mug in hand. She took a sip.

"Emma," Emma said, pointing to herself. "This is Micah."

Chiara nodded. "I am pleased to make your acquaintance."

"Why are you helping us?" Micah cut in rudely. He glared at Chiara, his eyes so narrow Emma couldn't see his irises at all.

"I thought you could use some help," she replied with a shrug. "Honestly, I've been trying to figure out a way to make these scumbags pay for keeping me hostage here for weeks now. They discuss the most mundane things. Can you even imagine?"

"Umm," Emma stalled, unsure of how to respond. "How did you get stuck here in the first place?" she finally asked.

"Went hunting for the beast. Ended up its captive for a while. Found my way to this village after I escaped." She shrugged. "Now I can't leave here unless I agree to fight the monster again.

Emma sat up a little straighter. "Wait, so you know what this thing is? You were captured by it?"

Questions slogged through her mind as her stomach growled. She wondered what the tavern had for dessert. She hoped it wasn't bread pudding. She absolutely loathed bread pudding.

"Emma?" Micah asked. He tapped her arm.

She jumped as she was pulled from her thoughts. "Sorry," she mumbled. "What were you saying?"

"I was saying that the beast didn't take physical form in front of me. Or, when he did, he remained tucked away in the shadows, as if afraid to show me his true self. I'm still not sure why he didn't kill me. I saw him butcher so many other people during my time captured by him."

"How did you escape?" Micah asked.

Emma raised an eyebrow at him. There was so much suspicion in his tone that it made her doubt her earlier sense of trust for Chiara.

"Honestly? He let me go."

"He did what?" Emma asked, dropping her hands onto the table and staring dumbfoundedly at Chiara. This representation of the beast did not mesh with how the men had described it. Maybe it just hated men.

"I'm not sure why," she admitted. "One day, it just stormed into my room in the dead of night and broke my chain free."

"Room? Not cell?" Emma clarified.

"Yes. He provided me with a room of my own. I still had to wear shackles around my ankles and sometimes around my wrists, but he didn't force me to live in the dungeons."

Emma toyed with a lock of her hair as she considered Chiara's words. It was possible the beast had a soft spot for women. Or rather, a specific woman. She met Micah's gaze. He shook his head, but it was already too late. She'd made up her mind.

"Chiara," she asked, "can I ask you a favor?"

"It depends."

"How would you like to face the beast with me and leave dear Micah, here, with Iris?"

Chiara's throat bobbed as she swallowed hard several times. Her cheeks flushed ruby red. Her fingers curled into a ball and then unfurled as she stared over at Emma with unblinking eyes.

A dragon tattoo wound its way around her neck. As she shook her head, the dragon shivered as if ready to expand its wings and fly.

"I can't go back to that place," she whispered. "I wish I could help you fight it. Truly, I do, but I can't go back there."

Emma wrapped her hand around one of Chiara's. "Shh," she cooed. "It's alright. I'm sorry I asked. I just want to protect my sister. At all costs."

Chiara nodded, more tears springing to her eyes.

"It was awful there. There were days when I never saw the sun or starlight. The sister moons never bathed me in a bath of silvery light as they crested the sky at the night hour. I was trapped. Stuck in a room with little to entertain. No one to talk to."

"I understand what that feels like," Micah suddenly cut in. He leaned across the table, his brown eyes soft and compassionate as he tilted his head towards Chiara. "I was cursed for centuries. Locked in a wolf's body, only able to become human when my master allowed it."

He reached across the table and took Chiara's hand in his own. "It is alright to be afraid of the shadows when you've been consumed by them. The scars they leave remind us that we are still alive. We are survivors. We are here."

Emma stared at him. He'd never spoken that passionately around her before. He'd been gruff and tender and kind. He'd been pushy and confident and sincere. But he had never been passionate.

He squeezed Chiara's hand. "I promise you this—when you choose to face your fears, to stare the shadows right in their ugly maws, and say, 'you can't control me anymore,' you will discover your own strength. Never forget that you are forged of fire and brimstone but also compassion and love."

A heavy silence fell over the table. A sliver of the barrier she'd kept sealed around her heart quivered slightly and broke into sparkling dust.

Chiara shook her head. "How can you possibly say that to me? You don't know me. You don't know the fires I've been forged in. Or how many cracks caused by being left alone in the dark were formed."

"That's true," Micah admitted. "But I know a fighter when I see one. And you are most certainly a fighter."

Emma gritted her teeth at the continued softness in his eyes. He was supposed to be on her side.

"Alright," Emma said. She cleared her throat. "So it's settled then. Micah, you'll stay here with Iris and Chiara, you'll come with me." She didn't care that Chiara hadn't agreed to go with her yet. She just wanted to interrupt the moment Micah was sharing with the other woman.

Neither of her companions spoke. They just continued to stare at each other.

"Well, so much for trusting you," Emma mumbled.

A tavern girl came to their table and delivered the bowls of stew and pints of cider.

"What was that?" Micah asked, drawing his attention back to her.

"Nothing," she breathed.

She didn't understand the emotions cycling through her. For the past six months, all she wanted to do was get away from him. Now, all she could think about was feeling his warmth on her skin again.

"So, you'll go with me?" she asked Chiara.

This time, Chiara blinked hazily at her before saying, "Yes, I'll go with you."

She didn't know what dangers would await them. She still felt like she could trust the woman, though, even with the uneasiness she felt at the way Micah responded to her. They needed out of this mess and quickly. Iris's life depended on it.

Finding Liam depended on it.

She drank her soup and chugged her cider as she listened to Micah and Chiara continue to discuss the plights of being imprisoned by a much stronger master. She wished her experiences with Grandmother Rel could compare, but they didn't. She'd been belittled her entire life. Beaten down by the unending ridicule from a woman who only wanted to take and take and take from her. She had hunted for them. She had fought to keep them warm in the dead of winters. She had taken the brunt of Grandmother Rel's anger.

But it still didn't compare to being imprisoned and forced to do the bidding of others without a choice.

She tapped her fingers on her mug as she considered what she was asking Chiara to do. To face one's darkness was the most difficult task of all.

But, when she opened her mouth to tell Chiara she'd changed her mind, Micah grasped her hand in his own and squeezed. She glanced at him, surprised. He shook his head, a sad, crooked smile on his face.

It was then that she realized she wasn't the reason Chiara had agreed to go. It hadn't even been Micah's words of encouragement.

Sometimes, facing the darkness was the only thing one could do to survive.

Chapter Four

Emma

As the earliest light of day broke through the trees surrounding the village, Emma hugged Iris goodbye. Her sister didn't return the hug. She'd become more and more comatose as the night went on.

Tears stung Emma's eyes as she whispered, "I love you," before pulling away.

Outside, Micah handed her a quiver of arrows.

"Where did you get these?" she asked.

"Stayed up all night making them," he said. He shoved the quiver into her hands. "Just take them, please."

She looked from the freshly made arrows and then up to him.

"Thank you," she murmured as she slid the strap over her shoulder.

"Anytime," he said before turning and walking away from her.

She watched as he hugged Chiara, then placed a hand on her shoulder and said one final farewell. Her stomach churned. Last night, they had stayed at the table long after she'd carried Iris up the stairs to the bedroom Fooks had provided to them. She hadn't slept well. Her head ached and felt as if it had been stuffed full of cotton.

"Are you ready?" Chiara asked as she stepped up beside her.

"Are you?"

Chiara laughed. "Yes, I do believe I am."

Emma raised an eyebrow at her. She had seemed terrified of going back into these woods last night. Of facing the beast again. Yet, even as they strode down a narrow dirt path, there was something easy-going and pleasant about her. She just felt trustworthy. Emma didn't know why or how.

Chiara guided them through the forest without hesitation. They were in a part of the woods Emma had never traveled through before. Although she felt the most at peace while among the trees, it felt strange wandering a forest she didn't know like the back of her hand.

"How much further?" she asked.

Chiara peered through the trees. Her cheeks flushed and the tattoo on her neck danced as the vein in her neck pulsed in time with her heartbeat.

"Not far," she said. She sucked on her bottom lip and for a moment, Emma thought she had changed her mind. But then, she set her jaw and her eyes grew concentrated and hard.

Emma smiled at her as she trudged forward. She had grit.

A large rock formation bubbled out of the ground like it was a fountain. Bulbous pillars supported what appeared to be a naturally formed dragon's head with its maw stretched wide open. Emma gasped when she realized the dragon's jaws turned into a cave mouth. Stalactites and stalagmites formed rows of pointing teeth as they entered.

"This is it," Chiara whispered. She fumbled in a pouch at her side before pulling out a match and striking it against the cavern wall. The light flickered but provided enough light for Emma to find a bundle of torches stashed against one of its walls. She plucked one from the ground and handed it to Chiara just as the first match went out in a puff of smoke.

Chiara lit another one and dipped the single flame into the torch. After a few seconds, it roared into life. As they descended, Emma couldn't help but imagine that they were willingly wandering into the dragon's gullet.

The air turned icy cold. The torchlight provided little reprieve from the frigidity of the descent.

They stepped into a large cavern with high ceilings. Pools of still water reflected the ceiling so perfectly that Emma initially thought they were giant holes in the ground until she saw the ripples brought on by dripping water. Crystalline orbs glinted in the torchlight. They lined the path forward.

"What is this place?" she breathed as Chiara pressed her hand against one of the orbs. Pink smoke filled it and spheres of light began to ignite all along a path through the cave.

"This is the beast's home."

"Oh," Emma replied. She had been expecting a dark tower or perhaps an ornately furnished castle. This cave seemed too full of wonder for it to belong to a beast void-bent on destroying everything.

Chiara took her hand and squeezed. "I know it looks beautiful, but trust me when I say that everything you find in this place was designed to lure you deeper into his lair."

Emma nodded, unsure of what to say. Paths branched off from the one they were on. More crystalline orbs marked their entrances, and she wondered if they too were designed to light up the path.

"How does it work?" she asked.

"What?"

"The light? I mean, I'm assuming it's some sort of spell. I've just never seen anything like this before."

"Ah, I see," Chiara said, "Well, I don't fully understand it myself, if I'm being honest. I found a book once—"

"He let you read during your captivity?" Emma broke in.

"Of course, he did," Chiara replied almost too quickly. "He's not a monster, Emma. He wanted me to be happy."

Emma raised an eyebrow at this. Hadn't she just said the beast had kidnapped her and held her captive. The hair on the back of her neck rose and a shiver ran down her spine. "Uh-huh. Okay. If that's what you have to tell yourself. Regardless," she said, "how does it work?"

"Well, as I was saying before I was so rudely interrupted," Chiara replied with a wink, "I found this book once that was written in Szarmian. I couldn't read much of it as I only know the basics, but it seemed to be some sort of science book." She shrugged. "It had diagrams of underground pipes that forced luminescent gas through them. The gas turns into smoke in the spheres and emits light, like what you see here." She gestured around the cavern.

"The Szarmians came up with this?" Emma asked. She trailed her fingers over the quiver Micah had given her.

"They're rumored to be some of the best scientists and inventors in the whole of Mitier. Why wouldn't I believe that they were able to produce the technology needed to generate light without fire or magic?"

On a whim, Emma placed her palm firmly against one of the orbs. She expected it to be hot, but it was cool to the touch. It glowed softly beneath her fingers.

"Why would a beast as terrible as the men made him sound install something like this in his lair?" she asked.

Chiara shrugged. "Maybe he got tired of the darkness."

The sound of clinking metal drew Emma's attention. She rushed forward, drawing her bow and an arrow as she moved farther down the path. She paused by a bend in the trail where the rock formations had melded together to create a type of doorway. She leaned in close and listened for the sound again.

Her breath caught in her chest. She could have sworn she heard sobbing coming from the other side of the wall. She held up her hand and motioned for Chiara to wait by the entrance. Then, she slipped through the natural doorway and into a medium-sized cavern.

She halted, gasp caught in her throat.

Bookcases full of texts and scrolls lined three of the walls. A round table sat in the corner by a small fire. Orbs of pink and blue light lit the rest of the room. A small bed rested against one wall along with a wardrobe.

"Who are you?" a figure asked from the shadows shrouding the bed.

Emma stepped forward, trying to get a better look at the speaker. Her face came into view.

Emma stumbled backwards.

"Chiara?" she asked. Sweat ran down her back as her thoughts raced. This had to be one of the monster's tricks.

The woman on the bed pressed herself against the wall. Her eyes were red-rimmed and her body was thinner than that of the real Chiara.

"You can't fool me!" Emma shouted as she aimed her arrow straight at the woman's heart. The fake-Chiara slid down the wall, covering her chest with her arms.

"Please don't," she begged. "Please don't kill me."

The real-Chiara stepped in front of Emma's bow. She scowled at her, her canine's flashing as she bared her teeth.

"Put your bow down," she commanded.

Emma stared at her.

"What?" she asked, too shocked to think of anything else to say.

"Lower your bow or I swear I'll rip your throat out."

Emma hesitated for a moment, but then slowly lowered her weapon.

"What have you done?" the fake-Chiara asked from the bed. "Arwawn?"

"Arwawn?" Emma asked, her eyebrows raising. "Who's that?"

43

The real-Chiara shivered and her flesh began to melt. It sloughed from her body like a snake shedding its skin. In her place stood a shirtless man.

Emma screamed, raising her bow, but not quickly enough.

The man shot out his arm and gripped her throat. His fingers squeezed into the tenderest parts of her skin as she struggled to suck in air. She choked and coughed, struggling to breathe. Her eyes streamed tears. Dizziness clouded her vision. Her thoughts.

"Stop it!" Chiara cried. She flung herself at them but was yanked back by the chain around her ankle. She wrenched at her manacles, trying to free herself from the wall. She wasn't strong enough. She reached out, her fingers barely grazing the man's bareback.

His eyes turned red and fangs descended, sliding over his bottom lip. He emitted the sour stench of old blood. She didn't want that to be the last thing she smelled before passing.

"Please," Chiara begged. "Please, don't."

Arwawn turned to face the girl, his expression softening. The fangs crept upwards, but were still visible on his ruby lips.

"She was going to kill you," he snarled.

"No, she wasn't," Chiara said. "She was just confused. You pretended to be me, and she didn't know—"

"She would have destroyed me," he continued.

The Chiara sighed, her shoulders trembling as she continued to tug on the chain. "She isn't a danger to us. Please, let her go."

He released a low growl and turned to face Emma once more. His grip on her neck loosened enough for her to breathe in deeply. It felt as if a thousand miniature swords were being jammed into her throat all at once, but she wasn't going to complain.

She was still alive.

At least for now.

"Swear you won't harm her," he said.

She blinked at him, unable to speak. She silently prayed to the Creators that he understood what she meant.

He quirked an eyebrow at her before dropping her to the floor with a crash. He stepped on her bow, snapping it in two.

Emma cringed as the shards of her bow scattered across the floor. Even though her heart hammered in her chest, she lifted her chin and stared the man in the eyes.

He gave her an amused expression before turning his full attention toward Chiara. He stroked her cheek with the back of his knuckles. Although the girl's lip quivered beneath his touch, she did not jerk away from him. Emma was impressed by her grit.

"I brought you back a plaything," he crowed. He leaned in close and nibbled at her ear. "I promised I wouldn't leave you here alone again, Chiara, and I shan't."

The girl closed her eyes for a long moment. She didn't say anything to him as she wrapped her arms around him and met Emma's gaze over his shoulder. There were so many emotions trapped behind those startling blue eyes.

She clutched at Arwawn's back, her long nails leaving tiny red marks on his flesh. One hand began to make symbols in the air. Glittering mist swirled around the girl's hand before forming into a ball of purple flame.

"Go," she mouthed as she pressed the palm of her hand against Arwawn.

Emma didn't have to be told twice. She bolted for the entryway.

He bellowed in pain as the flames expanded up his back.

"You little wretch!" he screamed, kicking Chiara in the gut. She reeled backwards and stumbled over her bed. Her head knocked against the wall with a dull crunch.

Emma didn't wait to see if she was alright as she darted from the room. She raced through the caverns, trying to remember which way they'd taken at the various forks in the path. She could only pray the Creators were there with her, guiding her through the maze.

Coldness chased her.

At least she'd found the monster. Even if it hadn't been in the way she had been expecting.

She needed to think of a plan. She couldn't return to the village without Arwawn's head. The men there would surely kill her, Iris, or the both of them. She couldn't let that happen.

Chiara's flames had stunned Arwawn, maybe even injured him. She considered the possibility of using fire to finish him, but quickly realized that wouldn't help her in retrieving his head.

It didn't matter. She needed to escape this place. To find help. She wasn't strong enough to fight him alone. He'd proven that in how easily he had started to crush her windpipe. She could still feel his icy fingers digging into her flesh.

She squeezed her eyes shut and kept running. She would either escape the endless darkness or die in this cave.

She could only hope Chiara had bought her enough time.

Chapter Five

Emma

Emma used a large rock to bust the orbs as she passed them, hoping the sudden darkness would slow Arwawn's progression towards her.

It didn't.

If anything, he seemed to thrive on the darkness. To seep it in as if it were a delicious meal. Wind rushed through the cave's passageways. The sound of his claws on stone thundered behind her. His presence pressed into the small of her back and bore down on her shoulders.

Cursing, Emma drew a dagger from her boot and charged forward. She didn't know how she was going to get out of this one, but she was determined to do so. Her sister's life depended on it.

A loud boom reverberated through the air. The concussive blast that followed knocked her forward. She cried out in pain as her chin smashed into the mountain floor. Her bottom teeth gnashed into her top lip. Hot blood seeped from the wound as she crawled forward.

She had to keep moving. It was the only thing keeping her alive.

Another boom sounded from behind her. She twisted her neck just far enough behind her to see a brilliant flash of white light before the blast hit her. She fell forward, but caught herself from face-planting again by falling on her wrists. They ached from bearing her full weight.

A ball of purple flame shot past her, singing her left arm as it careened into the wall before her in a blaze of glittering dust. She stole another glance behind her to see Chiara mustering up fireball after fireball. Her eyes swirled, glowing ever brighter the more flaming balls she summoned from thin air.

"What are you doing?" Arwawl hissed as he turned his back on Emma to face her.

Emma hesitated. She could stay here and help Chiara fight the beast, or she could leave it to her to defeat him. She wanted to help. To protect. It was her natural instinct.

But Chiara wasn't her sister. She didn't have a claim on her safety.

And she had told Emma to go.

She waited for a moment longer before leaping to her feet and dashing down the hall. Her stomach contracted with anxiety as she passed one and then a second bend in the path.

Her skin turned clammy as a thin line of blue light crept from her chest. She groaned as she realized that her body was conjuring her magical compass.

"Not now," she hissed, more to herself than anyone else. She shook her hands, willing the sputtering blue light to dissipate.

If anything, its brilliancy grew stronger.

"Balderdash!" she screeched as the blue light burned brighter. It shot back behind her and straight into Chiara's chest. She paused for a second, staring in disbelief.

And then she laughed.

She couldn't believe that, after all this time, her ability decided to act up when she was trying to make an escape. She supposed it served her right. She knew the right thing to do was to go back for Chiara. To help her defeat Arwawl.

"Fine," she sighed. "You got me."

She turned around and raced back the way she'd come. More balls of flame, these slightly less vibrant than the ones before them, shot past her. She assumed Chiara was running out of steam. She couldn't blame her. She'd seen what using magic did to both Grandmother Rel and Iris. Although she'd only felt the faintest of fatigue after using hers, she'd just assumed that was because her power was less physical than the others.

Her light was a guide through the darkness.

Nothing more. Nothing less.

She didn't stop to consider the ramifications of her actions as she slammed into Arwawl. As they stumbled back, she banged the back of her head straight into his nose before twisting around and kneeing him in the groin. He barely seemed to register the strikes. His body dissipated into mist before he hit the ground.

Emma landed face-first, her hands skidding across the rocky cavern floor. Skin peeled from her palms, leaving the stinging buzz of pain behind. She cringed as she grappled for her dagger and unsheathed it. Gritting her teeth, she rolled over and sprang to her feet in a seamless motion.

Arwawl rematerialized again. His eyes glowed a fiery red as he glared at her.

Chiara's fingertips glowed violet as she advanced on Arwawl. He smirked at her, an amused, yet somehow sinister, expression plastered on his face.

"You can never defeat me, Chiara," he cooed. "You need me, just as I need you."

Although her hands trembled, she lifted her chin and said, "I do not need you, Arwawl. Maybe I did once. When I was afraid of my wildfire. But not anymore. Not now that I know how to—"

"You think you know how to control your abilities? You stupid, insolent girl," he growled at her.

She shrugged. "Say what you will, but I know the truth."

Emma lunged towards him. She punched him several times in the stomach while simultaneously slamming her dagger into the base of his throat. His eyes widened and he bared his teeth at her. She yanked the blade free, and silver blood poured from the wound.

She raised the dagger to deliver another blow.

Chiara ran between them.

"Wait!" she pled, holding her hands up. "Please."

Emma staggered backwards a few steps. She couldn't believe that the girl she'd just seen shackled to the wall would want to protect the man who'd imprisoned her.

"No," she said, shaking her head. "I need to do this. He's a monster. He—"

"He's my friend," Chiara said softly. She ripped a strip of cloth from her dress and wrapped it around his throat. "You can't hurt him."

Emma's jaw fell ajar as she stared blankly at Chiara and Arwawl.

"You can't be serious," she said.

Chiara shrugged and linked her hand with his. "He's not always like this," she said. "Sometimes, he's good."

Emma's eyebrows rose. "Great. So, he's only a serial killing monster part of the time. Got it."

"He wants to be good."

"If you truly believe that, then you deserve to be together," Emma hissed. She'd had enough of this conversation. She'd come back to help this girl, and what did she get? The blue light emanating from her chest quivered slightly before extinguishing. She clenched her hands into fists. She didn't want to have to tell

Chiara she was a moron for protecting the beast, but she would if she must. Besides, she still needed his head if she was going to convince Fooks to let her leave with Micah and Iris.

"Listen, Chiara," she began, "I met you about two seconds ago, but I can't help but feel like I'm supposed to help you somehow. So, if you could just allow me to free you, then I can be on my way."

Chiara stood, staring blankly at Emma. The expression on her face made Emma's skin crawl. It was so devoid of all emotion.

She began to shake uncontrollably. Her face contorted into agony as the fire lingering on her fingertips extinguished. She swayed, her eyelids fluttering. Emma lunged forward in time to catch her before she fell to the ground. She sagged beneath the additional weight.

Arwawl removed the makeshift bandage from his throat, the puncture wound now nearly completely healed. He scowled down at them, his eyes glowing a menacing red.

"You think you can come here and steal my most valued treasure from me?" he roared. "You should have listened to the men at the tavern. They know to fear me. I am death. I am destruction. I am—"

"Dead," Chiara whispered as she lifted a feeble hand and sparks of purple ignited there. A ball of flame sped from her outstretched hand and into the middle of his chest. It exploded in a burst of flame and sparkling mist. Nothing but glittering dust was left behind.

Chiara shuddered a breath and went limp.

Emma sat in silence, cradling the now unconscious Chiara as silver dust fluttered all around them.

So much for being able to prove the beast is dead, she thought as she scooped the girl up and began walking down the path.

She couldn't believe they'd killed him. Just like that. Well, she supposed she hadn't done anything. Not really, anyway.

Chiara moaned softly as Emma accidently bumped her feet against a narrow wall. She tucked the girl's head in closer to her neck to protect her head as they continued on their way.

By the time she made it to the cave mouth, Emma's entire body was covered in sweat. She didn't care what anyone said. Carrying another person for what felt like hours was draining. Doing so after a fight with a nearly invincible monster was excruciating.

"Is it over?" Chiara asked. Her eyes fluttered open as sunlight struck them.

"He's a pile of silver dust," Emma said. "I think it's done."

Chiara shook her head. "Did you find his ring?"

Emma sucked on her bottom lip in confusion. "What ring?"

"The one he was wearing on his middle finger. Did you find it?"

"I didn't look for it," Emma admitted. "I didn't even know there was a ring to look for."

Chiara paused. "Did you, at least, hear it drop?"

Emma considered this for a moment. She tried to remember everything from her encounter with Arwawl. Although it had only happened a few hours ago, her memories of the fight were hazy at best.

"I don't think—"

"It's not over then," Chiara sighed. "Of course it isn't." She struck herself on the head. "Stupid," she chided herself. "How could I have been so stupid."

Emma dropped her to the ground and placed her hands on the girl's shoulders. "I know you don't know me very well, seeing as how we only met today, but here's the deal. I will do anything to protect my sister. And if that thing in there is still alive, then we have to go back."

Chiara shook her head. Her cheeks paled further, and she backed away from Emma.

"I can't go back in there," she whispered. "Did you see what he did to me? He'll do it again. I'll never escape him. Never." Tears sprang from her eyes and she turned away from Emma.

A thought clicked into place in Emma's mind. Of course, Chiara protecting Arwawl and then attempting to kill him made sense if he had some sort of ability to control her mind and actions. She scolded herself for not making the connection sooner.

"Do you know how to kill him?" Emma asked.

"Beheading. Fire." She shrugged. "Honestly, that's the closest I've ever seen anyone get, but you can bet I won't get that close again. He'll kill me before he lets me reveal his weaknesses."

Emma looked at her incredulously. "And what are those?"

"He keeps plants."

"Plants?"

"Yes, isn't that what I just said? He keeps them in a garden on the other side of the cave. He once told me that they were his most valuable possession."

Emma couldn't help but laugh at the absurdity of Chiara's announcement.

"It's the truth!" she clapped her hands together several times. "He cares for them dearly. Spends a ridiculous amount of time tending to them."

"Okay…" Emma sighed. "What else?"

"Me."

"I could have guessed that already. But are you sure he still feels the same way now? Honestly, you did just attempt to kill him."

"Yes," Chiara replied curtly. "I've attempted to escape before. I've never gotten this far. He normally kills whoever is helping long before now."

Emma threw up her hand. "So, what, you're just waiting for him to kill me?"

"It's not like that!"

"Then how is it?"

Before Chiara could answer, a blast of cold air blanketed them. Emma wrapped her arm around Chiara, drawing her tight against her as black smoke billowed around them.

Arwawl's took shape in the smoke, becoming more solid. When his face finally formed, he glared at Chiara with such venom that she shook uncontrollably.

"You could just let her leave," Emma said. She sounded a lot bolder than she felt.

He shifted his gaze towards her. His eyes were so cold, she didn't understand how she had been fooled by him to begin with. His fangs descended over his bottom lip as he snarled at her.

"Why do you keep her here, anyway?" Emma continued. "If you truly loved her, you would be able to see how miserable she is with you."

His upper lip twitched and Emma smirked. She wondered how far she could push him until he snapped. She gripped her dagger tightly as she said, "What is it? Do you delight in ruining her life? Does it bring you joy to see her tears?"

"What are you doing?" Chiara growled at her so softly that Emma almost couldn't understand her words.

Emma ignored her question and kept going. "You know what I think? I think you're a coward who doesn't know how to exist without inflicting pain on others. It's obvious that you hunger for the light even when you're condemned to live your days in darkness."

His eyes glowed. Emma deftly shoved Chiara behind her, such that she was between the two of them.

He lunged at them, his fingertips extending into long claws.

Emma trusted her gut instinct, knowing that he would stop himself from harming Chiara. She ducked just as he swung at her. One of his claws raked across Chiara's chest, leaving a thin line of crimson on her pale skin. Slowly at first and then faster, her blood began to seep from the wound.

Arwawl came to a halt, eyes wide as he stared at Chiara, then he howled. He whirled around and pounced on Emma just as she brought up her dagger. It plunged into his heart. He jerked as the blade impaled him, but clawed at her. Cuts coursed across her exposed skin and she became slick with her own blood.

She managed to get her legs beneath him and kick, flinging him backwards. He landed on his feet. He leveled his gaze at her and licked her blood from his nails.

"You taste divine," he whispered, closing his eyes for a second.

Emma gulped. Her dagger was still lodged in his chest. He had been completely unphased by the attack. So, the rumors were true. He couldn't be killed by traditional methods.

Beheading or fire. That's what the men in the tavern had told her would work. That's what Chiara had all but confirmed. Fire would be the easiest solution. She did have a firestarter in her possession, after all.

"Chiara," she whispered from the corner of her mouth.

Chiara shifted closer to her. Her eyes were wide with terror as Arwawl tracked her movements with his eyes.

"Listen," Emma said. "I need you to create a ring of fire for me."

"I can't," the girl cried. "I'm sorry."

"Why not?" she asked through gritted teeth.

"My powers are drained from the previous fight. I—" She trailed off and, for a moment, Emma didn't think she could continue. But then she said, "I wouldn't have enough control over them." She began to sob. "Please don't make me do it."

"Okay? What's the worst thing that could happen?"

"I don't know, how about the entire mountainside going up in flames and being consumed by my fire. You could die, Emma."

"Here's the deal, Chiara. You either do this and we have a chance at survival, or you chicken out and I die anyway because I highly doubt that Arwawl is going to let me live through this."

As she was speaking, he drew the dagger from his chest. The wound bubbled with blood for a moment before healing itself. He dangled the dagger before her, a horrifying grin plastered over his face.

"I was going to give you a life of luxury," he said. "You were to be Chiara's pet. Her companion during the times when I am not available." He snarled at her, his features morphing into something animalistic. "I can see now you were too strong-willed for that." He paused. "Your sister, on the other hand, would make a fine addition to my little family."

"Stay away from her!" Emma screamed.

All thought of survival slipped from her as she considered her sister being kidnapped by this creature. She knew Micah would never let Iris go willingly. He, too, would die trying to protect Iris. She couldn't let that happen.

"Do it!" she commanded as Arwawl flung the blade straight at her. "Do it now!"

Chiara hesitated. The dagger slammed into Emma's shoulder. Pain erupted from the spot and she cried out.

"Please, Chiara! You have to try. It's the only way!"

For a moment, Chiara seemed like a lost puppy, unsure what to do or how to do it. But, as Arwawl began to advance upon them, her jaw set and she turned her gaze fully on him.

"I won't let you do this again," she said.

He chuckled at her. "You're not strong enough to stop me, my little fire."

"Don't call me that," she screamed.

Her fingers sparked as purple flame danced between them. He continued to advance towards her.

"I hate you," she whispered as she thrust her hands outwards.

A pillar of purple flame exploded from her. It slammed into his chest, burning a hole through his center. He didn't even have time to scream as it spread over his body and completely engulfed him.

Chiara shook as more and more fire leapt from her. The flames formed a solid wall around Arwawl's burning body. He began to disintegrate into silvery ash again.

To Emma's surprise, Chiara bent down and ripped the dagger from her shoulder. Her touch was so hot it cauterized the wound. The blade glowed orange as the metal heated. She turned to face Arwawl, who was already reforming.

She strode through the purple flame. It licked at her skin as she passed through it, but she was completely unphased. She stood before the swirling silver mist where Arwawl's head had materialized.

His eyes held desire in them. And anger. But there was also a sliver of fear. Emma watched as Chiara spun her fingers over the blade, creating purple flame around it. Then, she drove it straight into his eye.

His face contorted as the flames scorched his face. His lips parts in a scream but no sound came.

"This is for my family," she hissed as she withdrew the dagger from his eye and plunged it into the base of his head, right where it connected with his neck.

Emma turned away from the scene as Chiara sawed off his head.

The air became dense and hard to breathe as the flames devoured the woods around them. Emma coughed, her muscles feeling weak and her mind hazy. Her eyelids began to droop as she imagined falling into a blissful sleep. A part of her remembered that she couldn't do this. She needed to find a way out of this mess. To escape.

To return to Iris.

But her body wouldn't respond.

Footsteps crunched on debris before Chiara leaned over her, her expression concerned.

"I'm not going to let you die here," she said.

The words weren't comforting.

Emma winced against her blazing touch as Chiara tugged her to her feet.

"Hold onto me," Chiara whispered as she wrapped her arm around Emma and held her close to her body. "I've never attempted anything like this before and it might hurt you a little."

Emma was too dazed to fight against her as pulled her into the purple flame surrounding them.

Chapter Six

Iris

Iris wandered through the dreamworld in a daze. She couldn't remember if she'd been in this part of the world before. She didn't know where she was going. Her heartbeat drowned out all other sound.

She stood in the middle of a town square. One she didn't recognize. People milled about. Their eyes were hooded and their faces slack. They didn't speak or look at her. Everything was shades of grey.

She began running. Was she moving toward or away from something? She didn't know. Her feet ached and blood seeped from cracks along her soles. Her heartbeat continued pounding in her head.

A pain wove through her side. She doubled over, placing her hands on her knees and coughing. Her dark hair began to fade to grey. This dream would consume her. She needed to get out.

She looked to the sky.

No sun. No sister moons. Only a sea of grey.

Her stomach churned as she stared upwards.

A hand gripped her shoulder from behind. She spun around, her hand instinctively going to the bottles at her waist. All those years of potion-making with Grandmother Rel had been worth it. She knew how to brew poisons and explosives that could incapacitate an attacker as soon as the potion's fumes hit them.

She gasped. Liam stood before her. Dark bags framed his eyes. Although he was still toned, he'd lost muscle in his chest and arms. His hair was greasy, as if he hadn't bathed in weeks. He didn't say anything to her. He just cupped her cheek, a sad smile crossing his lips.

"I will find you," she whispered. "I will rescue you."

He didn't speak but he rubbed his thumb over her skin once before he faded into nothingness.

Iris chewed on her bottom lip.

"Iris Valka," a cold voice said from behind her.

She craned her neck over her shoulder to see the crimson-eyed witch standing in the middle of a field. Her nostrils flared as fear wound its way around her stomach and squeezed. She did not want to have a confrontation with the Silver Skull coven. In a blink of an eye, the grey world was replaced with a babbling river and a canopy of trees. She rolled her eyes at the theatrics. She was used to the coven and their tricks.

"Crimson-eyed hag," Iris said.

The witch frowned at her. "That's what you came up with to call me?"

"You never gave me a name. I had to call you something."

"I see."

Iris shrugged. "What? No 'I'm here to kill' speech today? Honestly, I'm shocked."

S.A. McClure

She wasn't in the mood for small talk. If the witch wanted to kill her, she could try. She wouldn't succeed. Iris was a Spellbreaker. And she was determined to help anyone who asked for it, not be an abomination the way the coven thought she would be.

The witch laughed. "You may call me Edilda."

Iris's jaw dropped. She hadn't been expecting the crimson-eyed witch to ever reveal her name to her. There was power in names.

"What do you want?" Iris asked warily.

She scanned the surrounding woods, searching for any sign of the rest of the coven. She'd learned the hard way that the coven had the ability to physically harm her while in the dreamworld; they could kill her here and she would die in real life.

Not today.

Edilda plucked a starflower from the ground and twirled it between her fingers. Silver petals fluttered from the flower, dancing in the wind as they flew away.

"I don't have time for this," Iris said bluntly. "Tell me what you want, attempt to kill me, or leave."

The corners of Edilda's lips twitched.

"What, you think this is amusing?" Iris asked.

"Well, yes."

Iris crossed her arms over her chest and began to imagine waking up. She couldn't remember where her physical body was, and she didn't care. She just knew she didn't want to be trapped in the dreamworld with the crazy witch from the Silver Skull coven.

"I know you're trying to leave," Edilda whispered. "But I would like for you to stay. Something has happened."

Iris jerked her head up and stared at the witch. "What are you talking about?"

"We don't understand."

"Great talk. Thank you for explaining so fully."

Edilda huffed as she strode towards Iris and then gripped her chin between her fingers, forcing her to meet her gaze. "Listen to

60

me, Iris. Six of my coven members have died while they traveled the dreamworld for inexplicable reasons. At first, we thought it was you."

"I've never—"

"Yes, I know. But that doesn't explain what *has* been happening. There is a darkness in the dreams of so many now. It's as if the light is being snuffed out."

"What does that have to do with me?" Iris asked.

"We need you to break the spell."

Iris blinked at her. She didn't know what to say. First, they wanted to kill her because of her abilities. Now they wanted to use her. She didn't trust Edilda not to switch sides again before all was said and done.

"What spell?" she asked. It was better to know than to not.

"Honestly, we're not sure."

Iris closed her eyes to give herself time to think. For some strange reason, she trusted Elilda to not kill her on the spot. She couldn't explain it, but she sensed there was truth in the witch's words.

"How do I know you won't kill me the moment I've done this task for you?" she asked. "I mean, you just tried to kill me not even a day ago. My physical body is still weak from the curse you placed on the clearing."

"That was before the deaths," Elilda stated matter-of-factly. "Now, will you help us or not?"

"Conveniently, you avoided answering my question. How do I know I can trust you?"

Elilda smiled viciously at her. "You can't. All you can do is take my word for it. I promise that no member of my coven will cause you harm if you do find the curse, break it, and save my coven from whoever is killing them."

"And you would honestly leave a Spellbreaker alive just to save your coven? Aren't I supposed to be an abomination or something like that?"

"Even abominations can have their purposes."

S.A. McClure

Iris narrowed her eyes at Elilda. She didn't trust her. But she also didn't see what option she had.

"I want you to promise that you won't harm me or Emma." Her brow furrowed as she thought about all the people in her life that mattered to her. "You also can't do anything that causes harm to Micah and Liam."

"You would protect the man who betrayed you?" Elilda asked. Her tone was intrigued, but her face remained impassive.

Iris thought about denying it, but knew it was of no use. It was the truth, wasn't it?

"Yes," she whispered.

"You are a curious beast, aren't you?" Elilda asked as she released her grip on Iris's chin. She stepped away, giving Iris space.

"How do I find the curse?" Iris asked.

A bag of bones materialized in Elilda's hand and she tossed it to her. "Scry in the darkness. See the truth in the folds."

"I don't understand."

"You will," Elilda whispered as her body began to fade.

"That's really all you're going to give me?" Iris called after her.

"That's all you need."

Iris clenched the bag as she watched Elilda become more and more transparent until she wasn't there at all. She didn't understand why people kept asking her to do things she considered impossible. But, if this was a chance to relieve at least one of the dangers posed against them, she was willing to take it.

She cradled the bag of bones in her hands as she considered what to do next. Grandmother Rel never taught her how to scry with them. She sighed loudly as she sank to the ground and replayed exactly what Elilda had told her.

'Scry in the darkness. See the truth in the folds.'

She had absolutely no idea what that meant, but she figured there was nothing stopping her from trying. She dumped the bones onto the ground and flexed her fingers.

"Here goes nothing," she whispered as she scooped the bones into her hand.

She contemplated her first question. She knew from her training with Grandmother Rel that 'yes/no' questions were the best for finding answers. She just wasn't sure what she should be asking.

Sighing, she whispered her first question, "Is the darkness a place?"

She tossed the bones. They clicked as they landed atop one another. Hovering her hands over the bones, she waited for some answer to reveal itself.

Nothing.

She gathered them up again.

"Is there a spell to break that can save the Silver Skull coven?" she asked as she tossed the bones again.

Once again, the bones clicked as they fell atop one another. Still, she discerned nothing from their pattern. She breathed in deeply, her frustration mounting as she scooped the bones up once more.

She stretched her neck from side-to-side as she contemplated what to do next. Clearly, her method wasn't working. The first part of Elilda's words repeated in her mind. 'Scry in the darkness.' A thought dawned on her and she groaned. It was possible Elilda meant actual darkness instead of a deeper meaning.

dark abyss. No light. Not even a single star broke through its dimness. She imagined herself floating through that darkness, reveling in the sensation of nothingness.

When she opened her eyes, she was there.

She clutched the bones to her chest, whispering blessings onto them. She needed to break the curse so that she and her sister could be safe. So that she would be free to find Liam and rescue him from Grandmother Rel.

She cast the bones again. This time, she didn't ask a question. She commanded whatever force controlled the bones to reveal the curse. There was nothing for the bones to fall onto, and she didn't know how she would read them in the dark. All she knew was that this felt right.

The air thickened all around her. It vibrated with an energy she found both strange and menacing. It was as if the abyss were frightened of something she couldn't see. As if it were trying to warn her to get out while she still could.

She closed her eyes, listening for any sound of danger. She breathed in deeply, anticipating the stench of a beast trying to kill her. She'd faced them before and won.

She could do it again.

When she opened her eyes, the bones were glowing brilliant white as they twirled in the nothingness. They didn't land. They just spun and spun and spun until finally, they stopped.

Iris gasped as the pattern revealed itself to her.

There was no curse for her to break. But there had been an awakening. She sensed that the Darkness had gained momentum. The Light was fading. Images flashed in her mind that she didn't understand. A girl with dark auburn hair reading from a book. A lone mermaid, the last of its kind, clutching a glowing hammer to her chest. A man with many faces battling with himself.

None it made any sense. She didn't know these people and she didn't understand how they were connected to the Silver Skull coven.

She reached out to scoop the bones up again. The instant her fingers grazed the jawbone of a larger animal—she wasn't which kind—the air around her vibrated with such intensity that she had to close her eyes to stop herself from vomiting.

When she opened her eyes, six figures clad all in black, their faces hidden, stood before her. They clasped hands as they began chanting a spell. Warmth spread from her fingers to her toes as she realized what kind of spell they were casting.

It was a death spell.

And it was aimed at her.

Chapter Seven

Emma

Although the purple flames licked at Emma's skin, they did not burn her. She coughed as smoke filled her lungs, and her eyes watered from the stinging soot that landed in them. But she did not burn. Not even her clothes were singed as Chiara exited the wall of flame.

"And you were worried," Chiara said as she sat Emma down upon the ground.

Emma panted, sucking in the cool, moist air of the forest. She closed her eyes and wiped the soot from her face.

"Is it over?" she asked, when she'd caught her breath enough to speak.

Chiara tossed her a silver ring with a black jewel in its center. In the light of the purple flames behind them, it almost seemed to ripple with ruby fire.

"It's over," Chiara said. "He's dead."

Emma gaped at the ring.

"Where's his head?" she asked.

"It burned in the flame." She twiddled with her fingers before saying, "as long we have his ring, he won't be able to come back."

"Why didn't you do this before?" Emma asked.

Chiara shrugged. In the light of day, violet and blue bruises were visible all over her arms. Puncture wounds scarred her neck.

"What did he do to you in there?" Emma demanded. She immediately felt bad for asking. If Chiara wanted to share her story, she would. She certainly wouldn't want to talk about how she couldn't remember the days leading up to Grandmother Rel abandoning them. In her dreams, she sometimes wondered if the battles she fought in had been real. She also wondered if she had imagined the wolf who had been through it all with her.

She shook her head and smiled at Chiara, trying to let her know that it was okay if she didn't answer.

Chiara wiped away a single tear that slid down her cheek and returned the smile.

"I'll tell you when I'm ready," she said. "For now, I think we need to return you to your people."

They walked in silence for several paces before Emma asked in a tentative voice, "Where are you from?"

"I was raised in Forale before my wildfire became too unpredictable. My parents sent me to the Habith Academy for training, but even they couldn't help me."

Emma reached out her hand and clasped Chiara's in her own. "I'm sorry."

She knew what it was like to be shunned by the people who were meant to care the most. In her whole life, only Iris had been a constant. She didn't know what she would do if anything happened to her.

Her pace quickened at the thought of her sister. She wondered if she was awake yet. She prayed to the Light that she was.

She trusted Micah had taken care of her. Although she would never admit it to him—not yet, anyway—he was starting to grow on her. Still, she wanted to ensure her sister was safe. If the coven found her, even Micah could only do so much.

Part of her wished they had stayed at the manor house. They had been safe there for over six months. They had no reason to believe that they could ever be found or hurt in that place. Whoever had placed the protection charms had been one powerful witch.

"What about you?" Chiara asked, "Where are you from?"

Emma shrugged. She no longer remembered the name of the village she and her sister had been born into. "A cottage in the woods. My sister and I were raised by a witch."

"Oh?" she asked, "Not your parents then?"

"No."

Chiara shot her a glance but didn't press her for more information. For this, Emma was grateful. She didn't feel like shutting down the conversation, but she also didn't want to explain who Grandmother Rel was to them.

"What powers do you have?" Chiara asked. She smiled and said, "All I have is the wildfire. I wish I had something else, but that's all I've ever been able to manifest."

"Until just a few weeks ago, I didn't think I had any powers," Emma admitted. "The reason we were raised by a witch was because my parents left Iris and me to die."

"Yours didn't manifest until you were older?" she asked.

"Our parents tried everything to get our powers to kindle when we were young." Emma's lower lip trembled as a memory she thought she no longer had passed through her.

Her parents had let small fires smolder beneath her and Iris's feet as they begged to be let down. Iris had cried when her skin bubbled and the blisters popped. Neither of them had been able to walk for days.

She closed her eyes, forcing herself to remember the good memories instead. The ones of her mother reading to them at night and taking them to the creek to play. Still, the sour taste of a childhood riddled with trauma filled her with the need to talk about something else.

"I'm sorry!" Chiara clutched Emma's hand. "I didn't mean to bring up the past."

"Well, you kind of did," Emma said, forcing a smile. "Otherwise, you wouldn't have asked."

"True," she conceded, "but if I had known about your past, I would've asked about something else."

Emma's smile deepened and then she began to laugh uncontrollably. All the tension she'd been feeling over the past few months bubbled to the surface. They'd changed so much. And now, here she was walking with a woman who could summon fire powerful enough to destroy a horrible, monstrous beast.

To her surprise, Chiara joined in on the laughter. They shared a look, each recognizing the trauma the other had experienced and moved on from the conversation. They bantered and laughed the rest of the way to the village.

Micah greeted Emma and Chiara at the tavern door. He didn't say anything as he led them into the dining area and motioned for them to take a seat at one of the long tables. No one else was in the room.

Emma attempted to ask him where Iris was, but he silenced her with her a single look.

"Later," he mouthed before slinking out of the room.

Nothing but the ticking clock on the mantel and their own breathing broke the silence.

A door creaked from behind them and Emma spun around in time to see Fooks stride into the room. The same men from before followed him. They formed a line across the entrance to the dining hall.

Emma rolled her eyes. After all she'd been through, she'd had enough of the theatrics.

"So, did you slay the beast that cannot be slain?" Fooks asked as he sank into a chair. "Or have you come to tell me that you failed?" He looked around the room, as if searching for something. "I don't see its head anywhere."

Chiara held out her fist and dropped the silver ring onto the table with a loud thud.

"We have something better than his head," she said. She snatched the ring back up and slid it onto her finger. "This was the source of all his power. Without it, he can't reform."

Fooks scowled at her. "Do you honestly think we're going to take your word for it, girl?" He turned his hard gaze towards Emma. "I told you I wanted his head."

"Which do you want more?" Chiara asked. "His head or for him to not be a nuisance to you anymore? Because you can't have it both ways."

"Who the void are you?" he responded. His cheeks flushed red.

Emma could almost feel the tension radiating from him. He didn't like Chiara talking back to him. Well, good for her. She deserved to know how it felt standing up to bullies.

"I am the only person alive who was kidnapped by that beast, tortured by him, and lived to tell the tale." She picked at the dirt beneath her nails as she nonchalantly said, "Did you even know he'd infiltrated your men? He enjoyed wearing the faces of the men he'd tasted. Sometimes, he liked to tease them. Drink them so that he could wear their face and then terrorize them. It was like a game of cat and mouse for him. He was always the cat."

She held up the hand bearing the ring. "This ring gave him that ability—and more. He told me how it helped him focus his magic. How the stone in its center had been forged by the countless lives he'd taken throughout the ages."

"Enough," Fooks commanded. He held out his hand. "Give it to me."

"Why?" Chiara asked. "So you can attempt to wield his power? Sorry, but he I must tell you, he hexed the ring so that only he could use its magic. Everyone who tries will end up dead."

"You really don't know when to shut up, do you?" Fooks said, leaning forward. He jutted out his had. "Just give me the ring."

Chiara shrugged.

"Fine," she said as she dropped it into his palm. "But don't say I didn't try to warn you."

Fooks stroked the ring as if it were a precious item he couldn't bear to part with.

"We're settled then?" Emma asked.

He glowered at her.

"Yes," he said, then shooed them away.

Emma didn't bother asking for horses or supplies. She was just relieved he'd taken the ring in place of Arwawl's head. She pushed to her feet. All she wanted to do was see her sister and confirm that she was alright.

Micah gripped her elbow and pulled her to the side. He shot Chiara a furtive glance and then leaned in close so that he could whisper in her ear. His breath tickled the sensitive skin on her neck and earlobe, and she shivered. She fought the urge to step away from him.

"It's Iris," he said. He held her hand firmly in his grasp as he continued. "I haven't been able to wake her since you left. Her condition has worsened." He leaned into her slightly, as if his words were too much of a weight for him to bear alone. "I'm sorry, Emma. I don't know how to revive her."

She pulled back far enough that she could look him in the eye.

"Maybe she's trapped in one of her dreams," she said. It was the best she could hope for.

"Anything is possible." His brow furrowed. "We've always been able to pull her from her dreams before, though. This time feels different."

Her blood turned to ice at the thought of Iris slipping away from her for eternity. She was the only family she had. Sure, she'd made friends with the people Iris had rescued from the dwarf, Balkeen. And Micah was going to be difficult to get rid of. She liked Chiara, too. But they weren't her sister. Nothing could replace the bond she felt with her.

"Take me to her," she said. She shot Chiara a glance and shook her head. She wanted a moment alone with her sister.

Micah led her up the stairs and into a small bedroom. Two narrow beds were shoved against the walls with a table between them. Micah's bed was made, the sheet smooth and taunt over the mattress. Despite herself, Emma smiled. Although he'd been trapped in animal form for almost three hundred years, his military training was still so firmly ingrained in him he couldn't tolerate messiness.

Her gaze landed on Iris, and her smile vanished. Iris' hair was plastered to her skull. Her cheeks were sunken and her skin ashen. Her eyelids fluttered as if she were about to open her eyes, but she never did. Although she had always been slender, her bones stuck out from her body, her skin stretched across her frame, giving her a ghoulish look.

"How long has she been like this?" Emma asked. Rubbing her hands together, she tried to bring warmth back into them. It didn't work.

"A few hours after you left, she began shaking uncontrollably on the bed. Foam spewed from her mouth. I thought she'd been poisoned. I thought she was dead. But then the shaking subsided. She's been laying like this ever since."

Emma pressed the back of her hand to Iris's brow. She was cool to the touch, but clammy. She met Micah's gaze and saw her fear reflected back at her.

"We need a healer," she whispered.

"I don't think that will help."

She closed her eyes, knowing his words to be true.

"I can't just give up on her," she said. "We've come so far, together."

Micah caressed her shoulder. She gripped his hand and squeezed. She still didn't know if she trusted him, much less liked him, but he was the only one here who loved Iris.

"What else can we do?" she asked.

"We wait."

Emma collapsed onto the foot of Iris's bed and curled up next to her sister. She clutched her hand and whispered a prayer to the Creators that Iris would be healed. Her instincts told her something was wrong, but she knew there was nothing she could do to help. There were some battles Iris would need to face on her own. This was one of them.

Chapter Eight

Iris

Iris didn't know how she summoned the shield that blocked the death spell from hitting her, but she did. Golden light crystallized before her. Runes appeared in the solid wall that flashed brightly before absorbing the strike. The light extinguished as cracks formed in the shield before shattering into thousands of pieces, leaving her defenseless once more.

The cloaked figures advanced towards her in unison.

"Who are you?" she shrieked.

They didn't respond to her as they continued forward.

She didn't know many spells. Grandmother Rel had never taught her. Why would she? Iris hadn't exhibited any magic until six months prior, when she first began entering the dreamworld. Since then, her powers had grown exponentially within the realm of dreams. She'd once clawed her way out of a trap laid by the Elilda's coven.

She breathed in deeply. She didn't know who this new threat was and, in some ways, it didn't matter. She was a Spellbreaker. A Dreamwalker. She wasn't going to stand here and let them kill her without putting up a fight.

She imagined the golden shield of light reforming before her. Shards from the broken shield zipped through the air and melded back together. More golden light appeared, runes emblazoned within the structure as the light solidified into something impenetrable.

She delved deep into herself, searching for the heart of her power. It appeared as a small spool of undulating thread. Its color shifted as she tugged on it. It unraveled slightly but then caught. She coaxed it forward gently. She needed this. She needed to figure out what spell the cloaked figures were using to kill coven members. She needed to stop them from ever being able to do it again.

Opening her eyes, she saw that her shield of golden light had multiple holes in it now. Soon, it would shatter just like the first one had and leave her defenseless.

She stretched out her hand and began concentrating on finding the thread of power emanating from the figures.

A black, oily substance oozed from them. It reminded her of the way snow turned after too many days of people walking through it, little more than sludge. Although the substance felt foreign to her and made her skin crawl, she focused her attention on it.

The six figures used their collective strength to bombard her protective wall. Her brow furrowed as she concentrated on teasing out the threads of the spell.

She inhaled, letting the sense of it fill her.

She gasped.

It was a spell designed to trap dreamwalkers in this realm. To slowly weaken them.

She saw how it stretched out like a spiderweb, turning the world grey.

She'd been caught, she realized.

She saw how the six figures used the enchantment to track the witches unlucky enough to stumble upon the trap. She saw the layers of it. How they stacked upon each other. How her attackers could stop the witches from awakening.

She focused on uncoiling each thread of the spell. They were coated in the sludge-like substance. Shivers ran down her spine each time she mentally touched the spell. It felt as if poison were being injected into her as she teased out another layer of their spell. It was intricate. So intricate that she didn't know if she had enough time to unravel it. To break it.

She cracked one eye. Her shield was little more than a thin sheen of light now. Fissures crisscrossed over the hardened light. She knew it would shatter soon.

She redoubled her attention on unwinding each piece of the spell. As she broke different elements of it, particles of black goo separated from the spell's core and floated into the abyss.

Her attackers hissed as the last of the entrapment spell ripped away from its core and disintegrated into black dust.

She swallowed hard.

Her head ached as she breathed in slowly. A kernel of the spell still existed. It was like a gnat, swarming around her mind. She was too far in to stop now. Besides, she wasn't sure that she would be able to leave the dreamworld until she broke the spell.

She forced her way to the spell's core. It was a knotted bundle of threads, each one representing a different layer of the spell. There were gaps in it where she'd successfully destroyed elements of the spell. But there were also shorter threads where she'd only managed to lessen their effects.

She sighed, knowing she didn't have enough time.

Although it had felt like moments for her, she knew it had only been seconds. As she opened her eyes, her wall shattered.

She didn't have time to reform it. The longer the entrapment spell remained active, the weaker she became.

Instead, she imagined that she was in a small cocoon of protection. A thick, stretchy material coated her skin. Like the wall, runes glowed within the substance as it hardened into a protective layer. It wouldn't last long, and she would be able to feel every strike they made against her, but at least it would give her more time.

She plunged back into the spell she was trying to break. She clenched her hands around its core. Her whole body shook as she absorbed blow after blow from her attackers. She ignored the pain in her ribs, her back, and her legs. She thrust both hands into the center of the spell and began ripping wildly at the threads. She felt several of them snap.

Her entire body shook as the spell tried to maintain stability. Blistering pain shot up her hands, reaching her elbows, her shoulders. She knew it that once it reached her heart, she would die.

She didn't care.

This spell was unlike anything she'd experienced before. It was beautifully crafted. Powerful.

But also deadly and sinister.

She wondered who could have crafted such a thing.

She reached in deeper, grabbing the hard ball at its center, and squeezed. She envisioned it shattering into dust. She could see the way the dust fluttered away.

The poison crept along her collar bone. Its tendrils stretched towards her heart.

Blows from the six figures pummeled her. A hole formed in the protective cocoon and hot blood seeped from a wound on her left calf.

Her mind whirred. She couldn't formulate thoughts. All she could do was focus on squashing the seams binding the spell's core.

Until all that was left was a thin, sickly looking kernel of power at its center.

She let her magic guide her. Golden sparks sprung from her fingertips, electrifying the kernel. It began to burn her hand. Blisters formed on her skin and she cried out in pain. Still, she didn't drop the kernel. She focused on destroying it.

Her head snapped back as one of the figures landed a punch to her jaw. Stars exploded in her eyes as the air was knocked from her chest. Her grip on the kernel loosened as she nearly lost consciousness. She struggled to stay coherent. Another of her attackers slammed their shoulder into her chest. What little air she still had was completely pushed out of her.

More punches landed on her face. Her back. Her torso. Pain crept through her as blow after blow came. She couldn't focus on anything but that small, hard, burning kernel in her hand. She knew that if she were able to destroy it, she might have a chance at escaping this alive.

She squeezed her hand so tightly the blisters on her arms and hands burst. She screamed, her voice raw.

Everything stopped.

It was so silent that Iris thought she'd finally entered the void. Tears streamed down her cheeks, mixing with her blood. She didn't care. Her body was numb. The world had gone dark and she couldn't see a single thing.

A sucking sound enveloped her, and her body was pulled inward. Her mouth opened to scream once more, but no sound escaped.

A loud pop jolted her.

She opened her hand and the spell's core blew away in a cloud of glittering dust.

She gasped. She'd done it.

"You!" a voice snarled at her.

One of the figures separated from the rest. Her hood fell to her shoulders, revealing her countenance. Long, curly hair framed a heart-shaped face. Her caramel skin glowed in the particles of Iris's broken shield. Her eyes were the most intriguing thing about her. Blue and green mixed to form a tumultuous storm.

Her hand shot out and gripped Iris by the throat, her nails digging into the soft spot at the base of her neck.

"Who are you?" she asked.

Iris couldn't respond; the grip on her throat was too tight. She wouldn't have, anyway.

The woman sniffed at the air around her. Then, she dipped a nail into Iris's blood and tasted it. She shook her head.

"Whose bloodline do you belong to?" she hissed.

Iris stared at her with what she hoped could only be defined as defiance radiating from her eyes. She didn't look away as the woman raked her nails across her cheeks, leaving three scratches in their wake.

She shook Iris. "Tell me whose people you belong to!"

Iris blinked at her. Thus far, she'd been able to wheeze in a little air, but the longer the woman held her throat, the more lightheaded she became. Using what little strength she still had, she grinned up at the woman. She knew her teeth was coated in blood.

The woman brought her hand up to strike her again. Iris closed her eyes and thought of her home. She could almost smell the wood smoke as a merry fire burned in the hearth. Snow clung to the windows as the trees sparkled with icicles. She snuggled in closer to Emma's side.

Wherever Emma was, she hoped she would find happiness.

She hoped she would be able to forgive her.

She opened her eyes just in time to see the woman's hand come down. Iris's body began to glow. Her skin dissolved into tiny, golden particles.

Her last thought was of Emma's smiling face as she spun in the flurry of snow as it fell from the sky. A smile touched her lips as she completely disintegrated.

Iris's eyelids fluttered open. For a second, she almost forgot about the shitstorm she'd been through. She imagined she was back at

Grandmother Rel's cottage, before the attacks began. Before she dreamed of Liam. Before Emma almost died and lost her memories in the process.

But then world came crashing back down and it was all she could do to stop herself from melting into a fit of sobs. Tears wouldn't save them from this new threat. She didn't know who the six figures had been, but she was determined to find out.

After she saved Liam.

She didn't know what Grandmother Rel was doing to him, but she would make her pay for the pain she'd put him through.

The door creaked and sliver of light streaked across the floor. Iris sat up and rubbed at her eyes. Emma strode in, carrying a tray laden with a teapot, cups, and a few snacks.

Her gaze swept over Iris, and she dropped the tray.

Iris opened her mouth to speak, but found that her throat was too raw. She clutched at her neck, hoping Emma would understand her pantomime.

Emma nodded and rushed to a washing table wedged into the corner of the room. She poured water out of a pitcher and handed it to Iris with a trembling hand.

"I thought you were dying," Emma whispered as she sat on the edge of Iris's bed. She placed a warm hand on Iris's leg and squeezed gently. "Please don't ever do that to me again."

Iris gulped down the water. It was room temperature and had a slightly metallic taste, but it soothed her swollen throat.

She set the glass down on the side table and sighed. Emma squeezed her arm.

Iris jerked away as pain flood her body.

Emma caught her hand and turned her palm faceup.

"What happened to you?" she asked.

Gingerly, she trailed her fingers over the scars on Iris's hand. There were still a few blisters festering with pus. They appeared red and angry.

"Broke a spell," Iris croaked out. She gave her sister a half-smile that didn't meet her eyes. She knew she could die in the dreamworld, but she hadn't realized tearing apart that spell would physically injure her.

Emma shot to her feet and stalked over to where their packs rested against the wall by the door. She rummaged through Iris's bag, pulling out various salves.

"Which one works the best for burns?" she asked.

The corners of Iris's lips quirked. Her sister, ever the fixer.

"Green bottle," she whispered. Her throat ached with each word. "Purple label."

Emma came back over and popped the lid off the jar. She scooped out some of the salve and spread it over Iris's blisters.

The wounds instantly cooled as the salve began to sink into them. Iris sighed in relief and sank back into the pillows. Although her body longed for sleep, she couldn't imagine drifting off again. She didn't know if she could avoid being pulled into the dreamworld while she was this weak.

She did not want to go back there.

"Tell me what happened," Emma demanded as she laid down beside Iris on the narrow bed. She wrapped her arms around her and snuggled her head against Iris's head.

Flashes of the battle with the mysterious figures poured into her mind. She didn't know how to explain what had happened. She didn't understand it.

"The leader of the Silver Skull coven met me in the dreamworld," she finally said. It was the easiest place to start. "She offered me a chance to end the kill order on my head."

Emma hovered over Iris. Her hair tickled Iris's face as tendrils of it fell onto her cheeks.

"What?" She scowled, searching Iris's expression. "Tell me everything."

Iris nodded. Her head still ached, and she didn't know how long she would be able to talk.

"I only want to have to tell the story once," she whispered. "Will you go get Micah? I think he needs to hear this too."

Emma paused for the briefest of moments before rolling out of the bed and padding to the door.

"I'll be right back," she said before slipping from the room.

Iris watched her leave. She couldn't tell if she was relieved to be alone for a moment or terrified. Every time she closed her eyes, panic filled her. She could fall asleep. She could find herself back in that spot with the six mysterious people who all wanted her dead.

She chewed on her bottom lip. She wondered if Elilda knew how blood-thirsty the spellcasters were. She'd said six of her witches had died, and Iris could believe it after what she'd seen. The spellcasters were unyielding, bent on destruction. She wondered what their real motivation in killing witches was.

Iris focused on her breathing to. Dizziness kept her from moving too much as she stared up at the ceiling, waiting for Emma to return with Micah.

There is always hope, even if the darkest of nights, if you believe the stars will shine again.

She laughed at herself for remembering the line from one of her favorite stories as a child. It was a tale about Kilian Clearwater, the greatest hero Mitier has ever known. He single-handedly defeated Szarmian troops as they attempted to wipe magic from the world. He was the epitome of someone committed to serving the Light at all costs.

As a child, she'd dreamed of saving the day. Of course, Emma had always been the hero when they'd acted out the stories. She was the brave one. The strong one.

But Iris had promised herself that she wouldn't lose sight of the power she wielded now. She could break the bonds holding people back. She could save lives by extending her powers to them.

She smiled as she whispered, "I will be the shining star in the darkness for anyone who needs it."

The realization that she was willing to die in her fight to share the Light with others gave her pause. She knew it wasn't just words. She'd almost died breaking the spell tonight. And she knew she would do it again, if it meant saving another life.

She just hoped they could rescue Liam before she had to make that sacrifice.

Chapter Nine
Iris

When Iris finished telling Emma and Micah about the fight with the mysterious people from her dream, Emma stared at her, dumbfounded.

"Say something, please," Iris pled, taking her sister's hand. She squeezed it gently.

Emma sputtered, taking a seat on the edge of the bed. Iris sighed.

"Look," Iris said, "I understand that this is a lot to take in, but the really important thing to remember here is that the Silver Skull coven won't be after us anymore. We can finish our quest to find Liam without having to look over our shoulder every minute."

Emma nodded, but still didn't say anything.

"Micah," Iris said, turning to look at him, "a little help here."

She nodded towards her sister, who was looking paler by the second.

He placed his hand on Emma's shoulder, startling her out of whatever she'd been contemplating.

Emma met her gaze. "That's not entirely true though, is it? We may not have to worry about the coven, but what about the six people who just tried to kill you in your dream?"

She dropped Iris's hand and stood up. The room was tiny, but still, Emma paced from one end to the other. After a moment, she picked up a bow from the corner and began pulling the string taunt.

Iris watched her sister warily. She'd seen her like this before, but it always meant her mind was going a thousand paces a minute. Emma was the type of person who typically made snap decisions. She acted without considering the consequences.

But now, in this moment, she'd clearly devised some sort of realization that was too big for her to share.

"Iris, I'm sorry," Emma said at length, "but I think we have to stop looking for Liam."

What!" Iris flung the blankets from her and stood. Her legs wobbled and she nearly fell. Micah placed a steadying arm around her middle, holding her upright. She mouthed a 'thank you' at him before turning her attention back to Emma. "We can't do that, Emma! Didn't you hear what I told you? Something's wrong. I can't abandon him. Not after seeing him the way I did."

"And did you ever stop to consider that maybe this whole expedition to save him is a trap? Maybe he's not worth it!"

Before Iris knew what she was doing, she slapped Emma across the cheek. A bright red welt appeared on her sister's skin. The moment she'd done it, she regretted it.

"I'm so sorry," she said. Her head felt as if she were floating and she couldn't think straight.

Emma's mouth opened and closed. She blinked rapidly and Iris didn't know if that was because she was trying to stop herself from crying or if she was just trying to process what had just happened. Either way, it wasn't good.

"I didn't mean to," Iris said as she sank onto her bed. She cradled her head in her hands as she tried to keep herself focused on the conversation. The world swirled around her.

Emma's shoulders hunched and her face contorted into exaggerated scowl.

"Do you have any idea how scared I was that you weren't going to wake up?" she asked, her voice shaking. "Do you know what you put us through"—she gestured vaguely towards Micah—"over the past few days? We didn't know how to help you. We didn't know if we could. And then you wake up and tell us—" Ahe gestured incoherently and then sighed.

"I know," Iris said. "I'm sorry."

Emma laughed. "You are the most important person in my life, Iris. You're all I have left." She shrugged and then placed her hand over the mark on her face. "You mean everything to me. Do you understand that?"

A tear ran down her cheek and she batted it away as if it were nothing.

Despite the situation, Iris smiled. Even now, Emma was the strong one. She was braver than she could ever be.

"I'm sorry," she repeated.

"I understand that you want to save Liam. I do," Emma said, ignoring her apology. "But I'm not willing to keep putting your life in danger just to rescue someone who may or may not be working to kill us both."

Iris swallowed hard. Emma was right. They had every reason to doubt Liam. He'd done nothing to help them. If anything, the times he'd appeared in her dreams harkened danger. He could be working with the Silver Skull coven. Or this new threat. Iris didn't know.

But, in her gut, she did.

She trusted that he wasn't trying to harm her. She believed that he wanted to be rescued. But she didn't know how she could make Emma understand. She didn't have proof that he was on their side. And it scared her how close she'd come to dying.

"We can't turn back now," she whispered. "He's still out there, Emma. And he's waiting for me."

"Stars, Iris! You are so fixated on this fantasy of saving him that you don't even recognize how you sound. He is not your knight in shining armor!"

"I never said he was!"

"We're not children anymore, Iris. Just because we want something to happen, doesn't mean it will. If he really wanted you to rescue him, wouldn't he provide a roadmap or something?"

"He asked me to find him!" she shouted back.

"Yeah? And look where that's gotten us so far."

Iris quaked as she tried to control her anger. "At least I'm not so closed off to love that I push away the people who could make me happy!"

Emma stilled.

"That's not fair," she said, her voice softening, "and you know it." She stole a quick glance at Micah, who was steadfastly staring at his hands. The muscle in her jaw twitched when she looked back at Iris. "How can you love someone if you don't remember them?"

Iris shrank down in her spot. She wanted to provide comfort, but she didn't have the exact right words to say. She prayed that the Light would grant her sister peace of mind.

"You know I love you. You are my sister and you'll be my best friend for the duration of my life," Iris said, "but you have to let me love other people, Emma. You have to let me find my own way."

"But you could get hurt," Emma said, her face falling. "I could lose you."

Iris smiled sadly. There it was. The real reason Emma wanted to stop searching for Liam. She was afraid of losing her.

"Do you remember when we used to act out the stories of our favorite heroes?" she asked. She kept her voice light when she asked.

Emma nodded.

"You always wanted to play the hero. You used to tell me that you would protect me. Save me."

"I always was the braver—"

"I'm not that scared little girl anymore, Emmaleigh," Iris said firmly. "I have to have room to make my own decisions. To make my own mistakes." She closed her eyes, knowing that what she was going to say next might hurt her sister. "I need to learn how to be my own hero. You nearly died six months ago because you were so focused on saving me that you were willing to sacrifice yourself."

"And I still would—"

Iris held up her hand, stalling her sister's interjection. "Can we both agree that we want to save each other? That we love each other enough that we are willing to be each other's heroes?"

Emma met her gaze, a broad smile creeping across her face. "I'm not sure I know how to let you take those risks."

Iris shrugged. "You will always be the person I want to save me, but I need the chance to save you, too. We can save each other."

There was a long, awkward moment of silence as Emma stared down at her hands. Iris couldn't read Emma's face. She didn't know if what she'd said landed with her or not. She hoped it had. She didn't want to be a weak little bird who only knew how to accept help from others. Whether Emma liked it or not, she couldn't be that person anymore anyway.

"And you think that going after Liam is the best way to find yourself?" Emma finally asked. There was a note of bitterness in her voice that gave Iris pause.

"Yes," she said. "I don't know if I could live with myself if I let his cry for help go unanswered."

"Okay."

"Okay?"

"Fine. We'll do it your way," Emma said, meeting her gaze once more. "I'm in this with you, Iris. No matter what happens, we'll face it together."

Iris stuck her hand out. "It's agreed then."

Emma didn't hesitate as she took her hand and shook it.

Micah laid his hand on top of theirs. He cleared his throat before saying, "I'm with you to the end."

Chapter Ten
Emma

Emma cradled Iris to her chest as she slept in the tavern room. The small window in their room rattled as lighting lit the sky. She peered out the window. It was a glorious thing, the swirling rain and gusts of wind that carried debris with them. Streaks of lightning illuminated the outlines of the village.

Some people were scared of storms. Emma never had been.

To her, storms were a time when she saw the beauty of the world. The Creators had done this for them. Even in moments of chaos, there were threads of Light.

She kissed the top of Iris's head and breathed in deeply. She still wasn't entirely comfortable with the idea of her sister putting herself in danger, but she knew she couldn't keep her safe. She couldn't be with her every moment. And, with Iris's ability to walk through dreams, she would never be able to fully protect her again. There was always the chance that Iris would encounter something—or someone—in the dreamworld that could hurt her.

Even kill her.

Pounding outside the tavern drew her attention. As carefully as she could, she disentangled herself from Iris's arms and tiptoed to their bedroom door. Micah snored softly on his bed on the other side of the room.

Emma was thankful the storm was so loud. She hated mouth breathers.

She cracked the door open enough that she could see into the hallway. No one was there and all the candles burned low. Glancing back at her sister, Emma slipped from the room and silently crept down the hallway. She hit behind the railings on the second floor.

The tavern door flew open in a torrent of rain and debris. Three women entered, all clad in dark cloaks. The leader drew back her hood as Fooks entered the room. He wore a robe that didn't close fully over his torso and his hair was disheveled. He yawned widely as he stood behind the counter.

"What can I do for you?" he asked jovially.

"We're looking for a set of travelers. Two women. One man. Have you seen them?" the woman asked.

Emma narrowed her eyes at them. There was something familiar about the way they moved in unison. It was as if she had seen them before—but hadn't at the same time. She searched their faces, looking for anything that could jog her memory.

They were each beautiful in their own way. All young. All with long, flowing hair. All with a sharpness to their features that reminded her of Grandmother Rel.

Definitely witches.

She gasped at the realization. She should've recognized it as soon as they entered. All the signs were there. The way they moved. The fact that there were three of them.

She squinted at the one who'd withdrawn her hood, searching for what she already knew would be there. The woman lifted her arms to gesture at Fooks, her face contorted in frustration. Her sleeves fell to her elbows and there, on her forearm for all to see, was the outline of a Silver Skull.

Emma covered her mouth with her hand. She should have known when Iris told her that the coven had struck a bargain with her that it would be suspect. She should have recognized the promises for the lies they were.

She didn't wait to hear what Fooks had to say about the matter. She lay on her belly and crawled down the hallway back to her room with Iris and Micah.

She pulled to her feet as she crept through the door. She closed it gently behind her and then hurried over to Micah. Covering his mouth with her hand, she prodded him in the shoulder until he jolted awake. He drew a dagger on her before the sleep fully left his eyes and he met her gaze. She held a finger to her lips with her free hand before releasing his mouth. She motioned for him to get up. She began packing. After a moment's pause, he helped her. They let Iris sleep. Emma wanted to give her as much time to rest and recover as possible.

When they were packed and ready to leave, Micah scooped Iris into his arms. He held his hand over her mouth so that when she woke, she couldn't scream. She flung her hands out wildly and flailed her legs. Emma rushed to her and stroked her hair, attempting to ease her panic. It took several moments, but eventually Iris calmed down.

"What are you doing?" she hissed behind Micah's hand.

"We have to leave," Emma said. "The Silver Skull coven lied to you, Iris. They never intended to let you live." She paused, debating whether to tell Iris that the coven was here or not. She decided that honesty was the best route to go. "There are three of them talking with Fooks right now. They may already be on their way up here."

Iris's eyes bulged and her cheeks flamed. Emma didn't know what she was thinking or feeling, but she could sense that Iris was spiraling down a dark path when she finally met her gaze.

Micah lowered his hand.

"I am sick and tired of running," Iris hissed. She pushed away from Micah and tumbled out of his arms.

Emma raised an eyebrow at him, knowing that he'd intentionally let Iris go. He shrugged at her, a half-smile on his lips.

Iris rose to her feet and placed her hands on her hips. "You said there are only three of them?" she asked. "Well, I think we can take them."

Emma went still at the suggestion. It was one thing to know that her sister would be fighting in the dreamworld, but that didn't mean she immediately wanted to put her sister in danger in the real world. Besides, she was still weak from her encounter with the mysterious strangers from the dreamworld.

"Iris," she began, ready for the argument she knew was imminent.

A soft knock sounded at the door.

Emma and Iris spun around in time to see Micah crack the door open and then swing it wide enough for Chiara to step into the room.

Iris, who hadn't met Chiara before, lunged for a dagger that was holstered to Emma's leg and brandished it her.

Chiara's fingertips flickered with purple fire as Iris stepped forward.

"Who are you?" Iris hissed.

Chiara raised an eyebrow at Emma. "Do you let all your siblings threaten the people who saved your life?"

Emma rolled her eyes. "She's a friend, Iris." She laid a hand on Iris's wrist and drew the dagger down. "She helped kill a monster in the mountains."

"What your sister means to say is that we rescued each other," Chiara said with a smirk.

"I think you did most of the saving."

Iris twisted out of Emma's grasp and moved to stand closer to Micah. Out of the corner of her mouth, she asked, "What are they talking about?"

"Long story," he said, "but we don't have time for that right now."

"You should come with us," Emma said to Chiara.

"Is this about the three witches who are here?" Chiara asked. "Because that's why I came to wake you. I heard them talking about the three of you. Fooks sent them away, saying he'd never seen the like of you, but I don't get the impression they believed him."

Emma's nostrils flared. She was surprised that Fooks hadn't sold them out, but she was grateful he hadn't.

She met Chiara's gaze and said, "You really should come with us. We could use your help and it would be a chance for you to get out of here."

"We don't even know her!" Iris said.

"I do," Emma replied coolly. "And I'm telling you, she would be a great addition to our team."

Chiara frowned slightly. "It's alright Emma," she said softly. "I've been away from home long enough. I should go back. See if any of them are still alive."

"You can't do that," Emma said. She didn't know how to explain it. She just felt that her abilities had drawn her to Chiara for a reason. "Please."

Chiara shook her head. "I'll help you get out of the village," she said. "Make sure the witches aren't waiting to ambush you. But I can't go with you." She paused and stole a glance at Iris and Micah. "You have people who need you more than I do, Emma."

Emma close the short distance between them and took both of Chiara's hands in her own. "You've been through so much. You shouldn't have to be alone."

The half-smile returned to Chiara's face. "I'll be fine. Trust me. Besides, I really do want to go home. If I'm lucky, my family will still be waiting for me."

Emma wanted to argue more, to try and convince Chiara that leaving their little group was a mistake, but then she saw her sister's face and knew that it wasn't worth it. Iris needed to find Liam, and Chiara wanted to go home. There would be no middle ground.

Sighing, she said, "Fine, but I want you to send a message to me, letting me know that you're safe, once you arrive home."

"Of course."

"Not to break up this beautiful, heartfelt conversation," Micah cut in, "but we really do need to be going."

Chiara didn't have to be told twice; she turned around and, motioning for them to follow, strode from the room.

"Are you strong enough to walk or do you want me to carry you?" Micah whispered to Iris.

Iris shrugged. "I'm not sure," she said. "Honestly, I think I can manage, but I may tire quickly."

"No worries," Micah replied.

Although his tone was neutral, Emma could see the worry etched into his eyes. He really did care about Iris. Something about the way he watched her sister follow after Chiara made her hands twitch.

"Keep an eye on her," she said as she stalked past him. "I'm counting on you to keep her safe."

He grasped her hand and squeezed.

"Always," he whispered.

Outside, the storm raged around them. It was so dark, Emma could barely see her hand in front of her face. Except, of course, for when lightning coursed across the sky, as if it were splitting the heavens in two.

She held onto Iris's hand as they walked down the village streets. It was eerie how silent the town was. Despite the storm, not a single light was on in the cottages.

By the time they reached the town's gates, Emma was soaked down to her bones. She shivered as a gust of wind whipped through. She hoped they didn't all die from a lung infection, instead.

They had just stepped beyond the fence surrounding the village when Chiara spun around and made a strange gesture with her hand. It looked like she was trying to communicate something to them without speaking.

"What?" Iris asked, her voice carrying on the wind.

Chiara's shoulders slumped. She turned around slowly, purple fire dancing between her fingers. Emma stepped in front of Iris and drew her daggers. She wanted to use her bow, but with the wind, her arrows would be less than useless.

A vein of lighting illuminated the sky, revealing a row of six cloaked figures before them. Emma's shoulders tensed as she assumed a defensive stance and waited for the witches to do something.

"Iris Valka," one of them called. Her voice soared over the sound of thunder and wind.

Iris stepped forward. She showed no signs of fatigue as she placed herself between them and the coven.

"Elilda tells me you have broken the spell that killed our sisters," the witch said. "For that, we are eternally grateful."

Iris said nothing. Emma had the sense that Iris was waiting for the other shoe to drop. Something felt off about this encounter. Why would they come in the dead of night, in a raging storm, if they didn't intend to kill her?

"She tells us that she bargained with you for your life," the witch continued.

"Yes," Iris responded in a clear, confident voice.

Emma was surprised at how well her sister was keeping it together. She would have thought Iris would be quaking. Maybe she was and she just couldn't tell because of all the wind and rain.

The other five witches stepped forward. "We do not share our sister's opinion that you are not a threat to our way of life," their spokeswoman hissed. "You, who can break spells at will. Abomination. Spellbreaker!"

On the last word, all six witches raised their hands in unison. Tiny bolts of lightning passed from one hand to the next, growing brighter, thicker, and more erratic, as it jumped from hand to hand. Their speaker stepped forward and the lightning turned into a ball of pulsing, light blue magic. She launched it straight at Iris.

Emma lunged for her sister. Before her fingers even grazed her sister's head, the ball of lightning exploded in midair. Waves of heat washed over them.

Iris panted, her shoulders sagging as she collapsed into Emma's arms. Chiara launched a stream of purple fire at the coven witches. A wall of hard air formed in front of them, blocking the fire from reaching them.

Micah rushed forward. He spoke quietly to Chiara. She placed her hand on his sword and it began to blaze with purple fire. He didn't meet Emma's eyes as he sped across the space separating them from the coven witches. Iris turned her face to watch him charge forward. Her eyes widened in horror as a blast of energy struck him on his side. He groaned in pain, but kept running forward.

Emma stroked Iris's hair from her eyes and whispered, "I have to help him."

She charged after Micah, a dagger in each hand. The coven witches divided their attention between her and Micah. Blasts of energy, fire, and lightning shot through the sky. Emma avoided being struck by them.

From the corner of her eye, she watched Micah dodge the volleys. He leapt from side-to-side to avoid being struck by any of them. She raced alongside him. She began to let herself believe that they could make it to the coven witches. That they could kill them.

A pillar of lightning shot across the ground. Emma didn't notice it coming towards her until it was too late. Already, her arms began to tingle and she knew she was about to be shocked.

The pillar dissipated with a loud crack. She was thrown backwards and landed on the wet ground.

Shaking her head, she scrambled to her feet and then rushed forward again. She ducked low as a ball of flame shot at her. It singed the top of her hair. She jumped to the left as another burst of energy shot at her.

"Not today," she whispered, "not ever."

She sprang forward in the air and tucked her arms in tight as her feet slammed into the chest of the first witch. The woman shrieked as she fell backwards. Emma landed on her back but leapt to her feet and straddled the fallen witch. She didn't give her time to react as she plunged one of her daggers straight into the woman's chest.

The witch blinked at her several times. Her eyes widened as blood bubbled over her lips. Adrenaline pumped through Emma's veins as she whirled around and identified her next target. Micah was engaged with two of the witches. Purple fire formed a circle around them. There was no escape this time. They would either die in this fight or they would rise to the occasion.

One of the witches extended her hand towards Emma. Black smoke billowed from her hand and began winding its way around her middle. She swiped her dagger through it, but it just reformed. It began tightening around her, squeezing her ribs until they ached.

"Stop," she wheezed.

The witch snarled she continued to tighten her hold on Emma.

A burst of purple flame struck the witch in the head. The black smoke released its hold on her and disappeared with a gust of wind.

Emma didn't have time to recover as another witch raced forward and raked her nails across her cheek.

Emma didn't have time to recover as another witch raced forward and raked her nails across her cheek. She landed strike after strike. Blood began pouring from Emma's face, mixing with the rain.

With a cry of rage, she gripped the witch by her hair and yanked backwards. The witch cried out in pain and wriggled beneath Emma's grasp. Emma kneed her in the stomach and flung her to the ground. The witch flung out her hands and a gust of wind hurled Emma backwards. She slammed into a tree. Stars burst in her eyes.

Iris stood in the middle of the field, her entire body shimmering in white light as she lifted her hands. Her feet rose several inches from the ground and her ebony hair fluttered around her.

Chiara's purple flame snuffed out entirely, but so did all the magic wielded by the coven witches. The storm died to but a whisper as the shimmering light formed a sphere around Iris's body.

Emma shook her head, recognizing that her sister was giving them time to attack without the use of magic. She pushed to her feet and charged forward, drawing an arrow from her quiver. She didn't have her bow with her, but the arrowhead would be enough to incapacitate the witches. Plus, she still had one of her daggers.

Micah brought down one of the witches with a massive blow to the head. His sword wrenched free in a spray of blood. He didn't wait for the body to fall as he spun around and swiped his sword outward. Two of the witches that had been advancing on him from behind leapt backwards. Their eyes widened as they attempted to use their magic to no avail.

He smirked at them as he gripped the small hatchet in his belt and flung it at the one closest to him. It landed in her chest with an unpleasant squelch.

Three down, three to go, Emma realized. At least the odds were a little bit more in their favor.

Micah favored his right side, and Emma knew the place where'd he been struck was bothering him. She hoped he would be well enough to continue fighting. She needed him here to help her.

A blur of color drew Emma's attention. Her jaw dropped as Chiara crashed into one of the witches, knocking them both to the ground. She slammed her fist over and over into the woman's mouth. Her hand became covered in flecks of blood that dripped down her arm as she continued to drive her fist home.

The other witch leapt onto her back and tore her from her fallen sister. She raked her nails across Chiara's face.

Before the bloodied witch Chiara had been whaling on could rise, Emma leapt forward and straddled her. She drove an arrow straight through the woman's eye. Her lips opened and closed for a moment and then she stopped moving entirely.

With a scream, the witch who had been engaged with Chiara plowed into Emma's back, knocking her to the ground. She drove a small, silver blade into Emma's side. It glistened with her blood as the witch withdrew it.

Emma grunted, but didn't let the pain stop her from gripping the witch's blade hand and twisting it around so that the dagger pointed at her heart. The witch struggled to regain control of her own weapon. Emma met her eyes. There was anger tinged with fear.

"You should never have broken the deal struck between Elilda and my sister," Emma hissed as she shoved upwards. She wasn't quite strong enough to force the blade into her heart, though.

"Your sister is a threat to us all," the witch hissed. "Even you—"

She was cut off as Chiara kicked the witch in the back, driving the dagger through her heart. It protruded out her back. She slumped forwards and became a deadweight on Emma's chest.

Emma lay there, her heart hammering. Based on how relaxed Chiara appeared, she guessed that the sixth and final coven witch had been dealt with. She gave herself a moment to breathe.

They'd done it. They'd survived.

Again.

She really was getting tired to facing all these threats only to run into a new one. All she wanted was for them to be back at the manor house, tending their gardens and living their best lives.

Well, at the very least, their safest lives.

Chiara rolled the dead witch off Emma's body and stuck out a hand to help her up.

"You fight well," they said at the same time and then laughed.

Emma took her hand and yanked herself to her feet. "Are you sure you can't come with us?"

She knew it was a long shot. It was obvious Chiara had no interest in going on the quest with them. She didn't want to let her go, though.

Chiara sobered. "I'm sorry, but I need to go home."

Emma nodded, and they hugged one another.

"I promise I'll let you know when I'm safe," Chiara whispered.

"And I, you," Emma responded.

They separated as Micah joined them. He cradled his side and Emma realized she hadn't examined her wound yet. Gently, she pressed her hand to the puncture wound. It came back coated in her own blood. She pressed it back on the wound.

"You're hurt," Micah said, reaching out to her. He ran his knuckles along her jaw line.

"Just a flesh wound," Emma said.

She grunted as Chiara yanked her hand away from the injury and pulled away her layers of clothing.

"You are such a liar," Chiara hissed. She tugged Emma to the ground, forcing her to lie back.

"Where's Iris?" Emma asked, realizing that her sister hadn't joined them.

Micah turned towards the field, his eyes widening.

"I'll be right back," he said as he began walking away from them.

Chiara pulled a flask from her hip and uncorked it with her teeth. Emma cringed as Chiara poured liquid over her wound. Chiara summoned a ball of purple flame that illuminated the night sky as she leaned in closer to the wound to examine it.

"I think the blade was poisoned," she whispered, her voice turning to panic.

Emma lifted her head to examine the wound for herself. She felt cold. And her head swam. She laid her head back down.

"Is Iris okay?" she whispered. "Tell me she's fine."

She didn't hear Chiara's response as she drifted off into sleep.

Chapter Eleven

Iris

Iris wandered through the halls of a building she'd never been in before. She ran her fingers over the tapestries that lined the walls between doors. The threads used to create the tapestries were thick and vibrant.

She tried the door handles of the rooms as she passed. Each one was locked.

She knew she was in the dreamworld. She could remember the encounter they'd had with the coven witches. She didn't know if they'd gone rogue, or if Elilda had broken her promise to let them go free. It didn't matter. Together, she, Emma, Micah, and that strange, new girl had defeated them.

It had taken all of Iris's strength to block new spells from being cast. She hadn't even known she had that ability until she tried it. And it worked.

No wonder the Silver Skull coven was so afraid of her. If she could block others from even using their magic, she could disrupt the covens' entire way of living.

Music wafted from an open doorway at the end of the hall.

Iris increased her pace, hoping to find a clue as to where she was. She was wary, of course. She didn't know if she had the strength to face her attackers from before again. Not this quickly, anyway. It had been a small miracle that she had escaped the first time.

It was better not to tempt fate.

She needed to be on her guard for traps. The one resembling a spiderweb had been clever. That just meant that Iris needed to be even cleverer.

She pressed her back against the wall as she approached the open door and peered inside. To her surprise, Grandmother Rel sat at a piano.

At least, she thought it was Grandmother Rel.

Gone were her wrinkles and warts. Her once sagging body was tight with youth and her hair flowed in red-gold locks down her back.

Iris slipped through the doorway, then crept up behind Grandmother Rel and sat down on one of the chaise lounges. She waited for Grandmother to finish her song. Iris imagined herself invisible. She didn't know if Grandmother Rel had the Dreamwalker ability or not. She'd claimed not to, but she knew better than to trust her word.

Grandmother Rel played the last notes of the song and then closed the piano lid. She stretched her arms high above her head before rising to her feet and walking towards the set of doors on the other side of the room. Beyond them, Iris could see a garden full of life.

"You can join me," Grandmother Rel said, without looking back, "if you wish."

For a moment, Iris thought Grandmother Rel was speaking to her. She almost made her invisibility mask disappear so that they could face one another eye-to-eye.

But then, Liam's voice answered. "I would love to take a stroll with you through the garden."

He emerged from the shadows. His face was as gaunt as the last time Iris had seen him and, although he wore tight-fitting clothes that accentuated his muscular body, his skin hung from him where mass used to be.

He took Grandmother Rel's arm as she guided him out of doors and into sunshine.

Iris followed at a distance. Although they shouldn't be able to see her, they would still be able to hear her if she got too close.

"Have you found our little bird yet?" Grandmother Rel asked Liam as she led him into the shade of a giant willow tree. Iris stilled. Her heart raced as she waited for Liam to respond.

"No," he whispered. "I'm sorry, Myrella. She hasn't been in the dreamworld."

Grandmother Rel laughed. "She must not want to see you."

Liam nodded, but said nothing. Iris's heart ached and all she wanted to do was reveal herself. To run to him and tell him that she was coming. That she would save him.

All those thoughts dissipated as she watched him tilt his head towards Grandmother Rel and kiss her lightly on the cheek.

"You know my only thoughts are of you," he whispered as he trailed kisses over her cheeks, forehead, and towards her ears.

Grandmother Rel giggled as he nibbled at her earlobe.

Iris thought she was going to be sick. She couldn't believe what she was seeing. She had thought—she had believed—that he was in danger. That Grandmother Rel was hurting him. But here he was, kissing her. Touching her.

Her cheeks burned as she watched him lead Grandmother Rel to the willow's trunk. He braced himself against the tree as he pinned Grandmother between them.

Iris looked away. She couldn't stay here. She couldn't watch this. It was too painful. She turned to leave when a strangled cry broke through the otherwise whimsical sounds of the garden.

She turned back to see Liam suspended in the air. His arms were stretched high above his head and his feet dangled beneath him. Long, bloody lines formed on his back. Each time a new one appeared, he whimpered.

Iris bit back her cry of surprise. She still didn't want Grandmother Rel to know she was there.

"I know you've met with the Valka sisters, you insolent fool," Grandmother Rel hissed.

"I swear to you, I haven't," he moaned as another line formed on his back.

Iris didn't know how Grandmother Rel was whipping him. She just wanted to make it stop. Balling her hands into fists, she imagined breaking the whip that bowed him to Grandmother Rel's will.

"What can I do to prove my loyalty to you? Please, just give me a chance," he begged.

Grandmother Rel slapped him. He spat blood, his body sagging.

"Tell me where they are, Liam. Tell me, and all this can be over."

Iris held her breath as she waited for him to respond. She didn't know if he would reveal their location or not. She prayed to the Light he wouldn't. She just wanted him to know that she had not abandoned him and never would.

"You want to know where they are?" he asked, tilting his head towards her. "I'll tell you."

Her heart stopped beating. Bile rose up the back of her throat.

He'd betrayed her.

Again.

She shouldn't have been surprised. Hadn't he done the same when she'd released him from his curse and turned him human again? Still, that he had asked her to save him, to risk her life for his, and then betrayed her like this, left her feeling numb.

She released her hold on the lashings. She was too weak to break the spell anyway. Not after what she'd done to the coven witches. She sighed heavily as she closed her eyes and began the process for forcing herself awake.

"You will pay for that!" Grandmother Rel shrieked, drawing Iris's attention.

Thick, black blood covered Grandmother Rel's left shoulder and she held one hand to her ear. Her skin fluctuated between youthfulness and old-age as she healed whatever Liam had done to her.

"I'll never tell you where to find them, Myrella. Do to me what you, but as long as Iris is safe, it'll be worth it."

Grandmother Rel snarled at him. Her eyes glowed red and she snapped her fingers. Liam's body instantly went prone and he fell to the ground with a thud. He didn't move. He didn't even blink when Grandmother Rel kicked him, hard, in the stomach.

"You're still useful to me alive, which is the only reason I'm letting you live," she hissed. "If I know Iris, she will come for you. You forget that I am the one who raised them. I watched them grow. I nurtured them. Cared for them. And they owe me a debt."

She snapped her fingers again and Liam's body disappeared in a cloud of wispy, black smoke.

Iris's blood was like ice in her veins. When she looked at Grandmother Rel, she didn't see the person who had reared her. All she saw was a monster who only cared about herself.

Grandmother Rel had never loved them.

She never would.

She had only used them to unlock powers she wanted to possess. And she would do anything in her ability to manipulate them into doing what she wanted.

Iris couldn't believe it had taken her this long to fully understand that.

Even when Grandmother Rel had left them for dead in the mountain ravine, there had been a part of her that wanted to believe that it had all been a big mistake. She wanted to believe that the person who had raised them loved them.

She shook her head. There was no point in reliving the past. There was only the here and now and the future. Iris closed her eyes again and willed herself to wake up.

Her body began to disintegrate into particles of light. She felt a slight pull at her navel. She knew that if she opened her eyes, she would be awake.

"You can come out now, Iris," Grandmother Rel hissed. "I know you've been watching."

Before Iris had a chance to respond, there was a loud popping noise and her eyes flew open.

Chapter Twelve

Emma

The swaying motion woke Emma. Her eyes fluttered open to find that she was strapped to a person riding a horse. Hazily, she attempted to twist around and punch whoever was holding her, but she found her hands were tied together and then to the saddle's horn.

Her mouth was bound as well. She wriggled her jaw from side-to-side, loosening the strap until it slid down her chin and landed around her neck.

"Let me go!" she hissed as she pulled against her bindings.

A large hand clamped over her mouth.

"Shh, Emma, it's me," Micah whispered. He pressed closer to her body and said, "If I remove my hand, do you promise not to scream?"

His breath tickled the sensitive spot behind her ear, and she lifted her shoulder to get him to stop speaking to her.

She nodded.

"Okay," he said.

He lifted his hand and scooched back in the saddle so that she had a little more room.

"How are you feeling?" he asked.

"I'd be better if you untied my hands," she snapped, still struggling against the bindings.

"Sorry," he said. "No can do that this time."

She couldn't see his face, but she could hear the tension in his tone.

"Why not?" she asked.

"How much of the fight against the Silver Skull clan do you remember?"

She cocked an eyebrow. She honestly couldn't remember anything about a fight. The last thing she remembered was rushing out of the village with Chiara, Iris, and Micah. A storm had been raging and they were hurrying through the woods.

"Not much," she replied.

"That's what I thought," he said. "This is the fourth time you've woken up and demanded that we unbind your hands. The first time, you near choked Chiara to death before I was able to pry you off her. Thank goodness Iris was still asleep when that happened. I'm not sure what she would have done if she had seen you trying to murder someone in cold blood."

Emma didn't remember that at all.

"Where is Iris?" she asked. Her throat ached and she realized that she had probably been snoring. Internally, she groaned at the thought. She hated it when she snored.

"Chiara rode ahead to find a healer capable enough to extract the poison from your system." He paused as they rounded a bend in the path, his body tensing.

Emma recognized that posture. He was worried about attacks, and rightfully so.

"Iris is collecting herbs to try and stop the spread of the poison to your heart," Micah continued. "She's been worried sick about you. She's only left your side to collect herbs and wander into small villages asking for a skilled healer."

"Oh," Emma mumbled. Her head suddenly felt fuzzy and heavy. She leaned back into his broad, toned chest. His warmth pressed into her, making her feel strangely cozy and safe.

"We're not sure what poison the coven witches used, but if I had to guess, they used muldrock berries," he said. "I have every reason to believe that once we find the right healer, we'll be able to extract the toxin from your system and heal you."

"Symptoms?" Emma asked.

"Fatigue, mostly."

"And?" she prodded. "I feel like that there's an 'and' in there somewhere."

"And bleeding. We haven't been able to make your blood clot. Iris stuffed the wound with a poultice of herbs she said would help stop the bleeding and slow the poison's progression."

"Please don't make me tear every last shred of information from you like I'm searching for the lone piece of rice in a bed of cotton," she said. "Just tell me what I need to know about what's happening to me, Micah. I have a right to know."

He sighed and tugged her tighter to his body. "If we can't find someone who can properly extract the poison from your body, you'll die. Either blood loss or infection will take you as prisoner and never release you."

She nodded. She was dying. The Silver Skull coven had won in the end, after all.

"So why the bondages around my hands?" she asked.

"Every time we talk, you get absurdly angry and try to kill me, and that was after you tried to kill Chiara. You almost succeeded the first time because I wasn't anticipating the attack. After the third time in a row, we decided the best thing for all of us was to ensure that you couldn't harm us when we weren't paying enough attention."

"I see," she responded coldly. She wondered if even Iris had voted yes to this arrangement, or if it had just been Micah and Chiara.

Thundering hooves approached them farther down the trail. Micah guided their horse off the path and waited for whoever was coming to pass. Emma leaned her head against his chest and closed her eyes. He hadn't been kidding about the fatigue. Still, she couldn't help but open her eyes as the hoofbeats approached.

"Whoa!" Chiara shouted as she reined in before them.

Emma took in her frazzled hair and flushed expression. "What's wrong?"

Chiara nodded to Emma and then looked above her head to meet Micah's gaze. "How is she?"

"*She*," Emma said, "is right here and you can ask me yourself."

Chiara's lips twitched, but she kept her eyes locked on Micah.

"She seems more aware time around, but it's hard to tell," he said.

Chiara nodded and then looked Emma over.

"Where's Iris?" she asked.

"Went to find more supplies for her poultices," Micah said. "I haven't seen her in a couple of hours."

Chiara straightened in her saddle. "We need to find her, Something's happened to the west that we need to discuss."

"When you say to the west, do you mean Lunameed?" Emma asked.

Chiara raised an eyebrow at her. "What do you know about what's happening Lunameed?"

Emma shrugged. "Not much. Grandmother Rel heard rumors before—" She trailed off. She intended to say before she left us to die, but her memories of their trip to the mountain and their confrontation with Balkeen were spotty at best. Iris had described her fight with the cockatrice and her interactions with Micah, but those were still hazier than the rest.

"I see," Chiara said. "Well, I don't know what rumors you heard when you were still living with the hag, but what I have to tell you may change our plans entirely."

"Chiara," Micah said.

Emma could tell from his tone that he was anxious about something, although she wasn't entirely sure what.

"Micah?" Chiara answered.

"Did you find a healer?" he asked in a slow, deliberate voice.

Chiara rolled her eyes. "Where do you think I heard the news?" she asked. She reached into her coat pocket and pulled out a small bit of cloth tied around an object. "The healer me these and instructions on how to extract the poison safely."

She tossed the package to Micah, who caught it with ease. His hands shook slightly as he unwrapped its contents.

Emma scowled at what she saw: a black, crystal amulet, a poultice of sour smelly herbs, and liquid silver.

"I don't understand," she said.

"Once Iris is back, we'll knock her out so that we can work on her without having to fight her," Chiara said matter-of-factly.

"Wait a minute!" Emma shrieked, pulling on her restraints. She didn't want them to knock her out or anything else.

"Emma, this is nothing new," Micah said with a weary sigh. "We've had to make you unconscious each time Iris changed your bandages. Trust me. You'll be fine."

Emma slumped her shoulders. "You can't be serious."

Before Chiara could answer, Iris walked up from behind them and said, "I found a lovely patch of starflowers over by the river—" Her gaze landed on Emma, and she stilled. "Oh! Emma, you're awake. Hi...uh... how are you feeling?"

"I'd be better if you would take these bondages off of me!" Emma shook her hands at Iris, gritting her teeth.

Iris bit her lip. "Sorry, we can't do that. Not until I change—"

"Here," Micah said, tossing her the package of healing product Chiara had given him. "Chiara says she found a healer who supplied her with those."

Iris stared down at the assortment of tools and sighed. "I'm not sure what I'm supposed to with the amulet," she admitted.

"Grandmother Rel never used them when she healed people. Or when she taught me how to make potions."

"Oh, that's fine," Chiara said brightly. "The healer gave me instructions."

Iris nodded, fingering the vial of liquid silver.

"You know, the sooner you heal me, the sooner I can get out of these," Emma said, straining at the rope again.

"She's right," Micah said. "We should go ahead and attempt to extract the poison. If nothing else, we'll know if we have to keep searching or not."

Emma opened her mouth to agree with him when his hand clamped over her nose and mouth. He held a cloth in his hand that smelled like burning fungi.

She coughed as she drifted off once more.

Someone jostled Emma, and her eyes fluttered open to find Iris kneeling beside her. She was laying on a blanket on the ground by a fire. Groggily, Emma peered around the makeshift camp and sighed. She was surprised Micah hadn't taken the time to get it military ready. He was normally so fastidious when it came to following regulation.

Iris pressed a cold hand to Emma's brow and counted to ten. She frowned as she withdrew her hand.

"You're still running a fever," she said, concern in her voice.

"Okay?" Emma said. She wasn't sure what the big deal was. She rarely got sick and she was confident she would be able to fight off whatever had her in bed.

"What's the last thing you remember?" Iris asked as she peered into her eyes.

Emma's brow furrowed as she thought back on the past several days. She frowned when she got to the part with the witch stabbing her in the side and then there was nothing but blank space.

"Some cloaked witch stuck me with a dagger," she said, and then waited to see her sister's reaction.

Iris chewed on her bottom lip, her eyes wide.

"Well, you remember more than last time, so I supposed that's a good thing," she finally said. "And, thanks be the Creators, the bleeding has stopped." She paused and her expression fell. "I just don't know if we extracted all the poison or not. You've had a fever ever since we performed the spell."

"Is she awake?" Chiara asked. She bent over Iris to peer into Emma's face. Although her tone was rough, her expression was etched with concern. "How are you feeling?"

"Honestly, I'd feel a lot better if you both could give me some space." Emma tried to wave her hand at them, but found her wrists were bound together.

They backed away and relief immediately filled Emma. She sat up. Her neck was a little stiff, but other than that, she felt great. She smiled at them and lifted her hands.

"Now, can I finally get these ropes taken off?" she asked.

"Of course," Iris said. She pulled a small dagger from the belt at her hip and sliced the ropes free. Silver lined her eyes when she drew back from Emma and she turned away quickly.

"How long have I been ill?" Emma asked, rubbing the raw, swollen skin from where the rope had chafed against her.

"Days," Chiara replied vaguely. "We've been moving at a glacial pace, trying to keep you from injuring yourself or one of us. Trying to keep you from dying." She squared her shoulders. "But you're fine now. Or, at the very least, you're on your way to recovery."

Micah came over with a small bowl of soup and handed it to her. He didn't say anything as she accepted it. She started to thank him, but he hurried away.

She watched as he disappeared outside the tent. She had the vague sense that he had done most of the protecting while she had been out of commission.

Hazy memories flitted through her mind. None of them made any sense. Most of them were of her flailing against one, two, or all three of her friends as they tried to sedate her. She grimaced as she remembered one particular instance in which she slammed her palm straight in Iris's nose. Blood had gushed from her sister's nostrils before she'd succumbed to sleep once more..

"I'm sorry," she whispered to her sister.

"For what?"

"You know, breaking your nose."

Iris leaned away from her, her eyes wide and her cheeks flushed. "You remember that?"

"Yes."

"That's good to hear," Chiara broke in. "We were worried you wouldn't remember all the nasty, horrible things you did to us while you were poisoned." She smiled. "Now we can make you feel bad for the rest of your days."

A thought occurred to Emma. "Weren't you going home?" she asked. "To find your family?"

Chiara shrugged. "Once you were hurt, it seemed like they needed me more here than my family does. So, I stayed."

"I'm glad you did," Emma said, a smile spreading across her face.

"You might not feel that way once I tell you what I heard when I was collecting the medicine to heal you," she replied.

"Are you finally going to tell us?" Micah asked as he re-entered the tent. He tilted his head towards Chiara, an eager expression on his face.

Emma pulled her legs up to her chest and wrapped her arms around them as she waited for Chiara to explain what she'd heard.

"Everyone was discussing it," Chiara began. "The rumors are that Prince Fredrick and Princess Saphria will make an announcement soon that they will want every able-bodied magic-wielder to help in the war."

"War?" Iris asked, crinkling her nose. "What war, Chiara?"

"The war to the west, of course. In Lunameed."

"What are you talking about?" Micah and Iris asked at the same time.

Chiara sighed. "I'm sure you heard that King Magnus proposed to his own daughter."

Iris and Emma shared a look. They had heard that rumor months ago when they were still living with Grandmother Rel.

"Yes," they replied in unison.

"Well, Princess Amaleah declared war against him. She said that he wasn't fit to rule her kingdom."

Emma's jaw dropped. She'd never heard of a princess waging war against her own father to claim the crown. Of course, it was rare for princes to do that, either.

Chiara turned to look at Micah. "Prince Colin of Szarmi is rumored to be in their number. And the elves. And the centaurs."

"A Szarmian prince and a Lunameedian princess," Iris whispered. "Who would have thought they'd ever work together. I thought their kingdoms hated one another."

"Oh, they do," Chiara said. "But apparently, they've come to some sort of agreement about helping each other fight for their respective kingdoms."

Emma took in what Chiara was saying without much to add. It was difficult to process. And she didn't see how any of that information had an impact on her.

"We have to answer the royals' call," Chiara said, as if reading her confusion. "We have to."

Iris shook her head. "What do you mean, we have to? I already told you once, but it seems like I need to say it again, I am not abandoning Liam to be Grandmother Rel's little toy."

"But things have changed now," Chiara pressed. "Can't you see that? It's not just about the war brewing in Lunameed or their princess's rebellion. There's been talk of a darkness spreading across the land for decades. Even centuries, if you talk to some of the elders. I know what it was liking living with a creature consumed by Darkness." Her eyes glistened with silver as she spoke, and her hand gestures became more animated. "It might be time for the followers of the Light to take a stand. We have to do something!"

Iris scowled.

"No," she whispered. "We don't have to do anything. I'm here for one reason and one reason only— to save Liam. After I find him and rescue him, maybe then we'll join the fight, but not before."

"Iris, you have to be reasonable," Chiara said, pleadingly. "You can't honestly intend to base all your decisions on Liam for the foreseeable future. Didn't you tell us that the last time you saw him, he appeared happy to be with Grandmother Rel?"

"Until she began torturing him!" Iris snarled. "And, you forget that Grandmother Rel knew I was watching. I think she wanted to send me a message. Come get him, or else."

"Alright. Let's all just calm down," Emma said, raising her hands in what she hoped was a placating way. "Iris, I know how much you want to save Liam, but if the royal family is asking for help, maybe we should go."

Iris stared at her for a long moment. She didn't speak. She barely blinked.

"Say something," Emma commanded.

Iris looked away from her then. Silver lined her eyes, but the rest of her face was expressionless.

Emma's heart began pounding in her chest. She'd rarely seen her sister respond like this. Normally, Iris was calm and collected when having discussions. But, like everything else dealing with Liam, she had been emotional and erratic.

"Iris, please, we have to at least consider—" Emma broke off when Iris suddenly leapt to her feet and stormed away.

Chapter Thirteen

Iris

Iris held the tears back until she was out of earshot of her friends
and sister. She went into the woods behind their tent. She knew
Emma's words had merit. She understood that, especially with
her ability as a Spellbreaker, she needed to focus on the good of
all, and not just the good of one.

It didn't change the fact that every time she closed her eyes,
she saw Liam's face. She saw the wounds Grandmother Rel
inflicted upon him. She felt his heartache. Smelled his fear.

He needed her help.

She picked up a fallen branch and walloped one of the trees
with it until the palms of her hands had turned red and ached from

gripping it so hard. She dropped the branch, then sank onto a log, placing her head in her hands. She sobbed until her body shook.

A low thud drew her attention. She scrambled to unsheath her dagger from its holster on her belt. Tilting her head, she listened for the thud to sound again.

It did. Closer. Louder.

Her body jostled with it.

Clenching her jaw, she rose to her feet and crept back the way she'd come. She prayed to the Creators that whatever was in the woods with her would remain there.

She stilled when, in the distance, two pinpricks of purple light shone through the darkness. They blinked.

Whatever it was, it was alive.

Iris turned tail and ran as fast as she could towards the camp.

Loud booms shook the earth around her, and she screamed. The creature, whatever it was, was getting closer. She ducked beneath a low hanging branch. In her haste, she didn't notice the large root protruding from the ground until she tripped on it. She tumbled face-first to the ground. Her jaw hit another root and the coppery taste of blood filled her mouth.

Groaning, she stumbled to her feet. The booming was louder. The ground shook more violently beneath her feet as she continued onward. She screamed for help, but the booming was so loud, it drowned out any response that might have come.

She threw out hands, grasping for any sign that a spell had been cast that she could break. There was nothing.

Pumping her legs faster, she increased her speed enough to outpace the creature for a few moments. She stole a glance behind her. There were now five sets of purple eyes.

"Void!" she screamed as she leapt over another upturned root. She ignored the pain in her knees and calves. If she stopped, she knew it would mean death.

"Iris?" Emma called from in front of her.

In that moment, it didn't matter that she was angry with her sister. All that mattered was getting away from the creature.

S.A. McClure

"Run!" she screamed. She tugged on Emma's hand as she passed her.

"What's going on?" Emma asked.

"Monsters. Behind. Us," Iris said in gasps. A stitch formed in her side. All she wanted to do was stop running.

Emma shoved her forward.

"Whatever you hear, don't keep running," she said as she released Iris's hand.

Iris cranked her head around in time to see Emma square her shoulders and turn to face whatever monster was chasing her.

"To void you are!" Iris screamed, skidding to a halt. "Emma, you've barely recovered from the poison!" She sprinted back to her sister and yanked on her arm. "Please, Emma!"

Emma leaned over and kissed Iris on the brow.

"You have always been the best of us," she whispered as she slipped out of Iris's grasp and advanced towards the monsters.

"That's such malarkey!" Iris yelled. She didn't hesitate as she trailed after her sister. "You and me together. That's the deal, Emma. You can't break it. I won't let you."

Emma drew her daggers with shaking arms.

"Whatever happens," she whispered, "I love you."

"Don't make it sound like we're dying today, Emma," Iris chided. "I am determined that we can survive this."

She pointed her dagger towards the quickly approaching sets of purple eyes.

Dirt sprayed across their faces as something massive fell to the ground in front of them. She shook as she cracked her eyes open.

A large, rocky figure stood before her. It's glowing, purple eyes blinked down at her. It had a round head and a crude joint between its lower mandible and its upper.

Iris cocked her head at it. "It's so ugly, it's kind of adorable, isn't it?"

The creature bent down low so that it was nearly eye-level with Iris. It was massive. At least three times as tall as she was and bulky. She quivered slightly beneath its stare.

"Emma?" she asked from the corner of her mouth.

The creature nudged her with its lower jaw.

"Emma!" she said again, a little more forcibly.

The creature reared back, its face taking an angry tone as it slammed its fists down into the ground. The whole world seemed to shake as dirt flew into the air and trees shuddered loose and fell. When the dust settled, a giant hole was in the ground in front of them.

Her hands shook as she turned to look at Emma. Her face was paler than it ever had been before.

Emma took her hand and practically dragged her back towards the camp.

The rock monster and its companions continued their pursuit of them.

"What are those things?" Emma huffed.

Normally, this type of run wouldn't have winded her, but since she'd been bed-ridden for the past several weeks, Iris supposed she'd lost some of her stamina.

"I have no idea!" Iris replied. The stitch in her side began pulling again and she laid her free hand on top of it.

"You alright?" Emma asked.

"I will be if we can get away from these things."

Purple fire sprang to life behind them. Iris smiled in relief. It was the push she needed to propel herself forward.

The rock monster swiped a hand through the dirt, smothering the flames. It roared as Chiara released another volley, straight for its heart.

"Micah heard the booms and was packing up camp. The horses are ready," she said as she maintained the stream of fire. "Just go!"

She dug in her feet as she expanded the reach of her flames. They leapt from tree to tree, creating a wild, raging fire. Sweat dripped down her brow and she gritted her teeth.

Iris met her gaze. "You know we can't leave you here alone to fight against these things."

"Where did the golems come from?" Chiara asked.

S.A. McClure

"Is that what they are?" Iris asked. "I was calling them rock monsters."

Chiara glanced at her, strained expression in place, and Iris laughed nervously.

"I'm not sure where they came from. One moment, I was sitting by myself in the woods. The next, boom, there they were." She sucked in a deep breath and then said, "Emma can't fight. Not yet, anyway. She's still too weak."

"I'm standing right here," Emma snapped.

"If it's the truth, then there's no reason to be insulted," Chiara said.

"Thank you for the support," Emma seethed.

At that moment, Chiara's fire burned out and she slumped to the ground. The golems roared as they piled dirt on the flames, stifling them.

Together, Iris and Emma wrapped their arms under Chiara's shoulders. They hefted her to her feet and then supported her as they fled towards the camp.

"Chiara, what do you know about golems?" Iris asked.

"Just the basics," she said. "Mud and rock monsters controlled by someone else."

Iris jerked her head towards Chiara. "What do you mean, 'controlled by someone else?'"

"Just what I said. If I remember correctly, someone has to forge them out of clay and the only way to destroy them is to shatter the smaller versions."

"How do we know where their smaller versions are?" she asked.

They entered the soft glow of the campfire. Micah had already packed and loaded their belongings on their horses.

He turned around and rushed towards them. He scooped her into his arms. Surprisingly, she didn't fight against him as he placed her in his saddle and then climbed on behind her.

Iris laid a hand on Chiara's shoulder. "Is there anything else you can tell me about them?"

"Honestly, I'm not sure what kind of information you're looking for," she said, panting. "I'm sorry. I don't remember much."

"Honestly, what you've told me just now is enough," she said.

An idea spawned in her. She whirled on Emma.

"I need your help," she said frantically.

Chapter Fourteen

Iris

Iris gripped Emma's hand firmly in hers. Every nerve-ending within her vibrated as she contemplated what she was about to attempt. She didn't know if she was strong enough to pull her sister into the dreamworld with her. She didn't even know if Emma's ability to find people would work in the dreamworld.

But it was the only thing she could think of that had the potential to save them from the golems.

"Are you ready?" she asked, squeezing her sister's hand.

Emma nodded, though her face was peaked and her eyes had agleam to them.

"It's not so bad," Iris said, comfortingly.

"You forget that I watched you wander this dreamworld once before, with Grandmother Rel," Emma replied with too much cockiness.

"It's okay to be nervous," Iris said.

"I'm not," Emma said defensively.

Iris closed her eyes and sighed as she let her mind drift towards the dreamworld. She'd entered it so often that she slipped into it seamlessly. The only difference this time was that she tethered herself to Emma.

When she opened her eyes, she was standing in the middle of a beach. Waves crashed soothingly and the sister moons loomed above them, illuminating the water's surface.

She breathed in the salty air. This was new. Normally, she landed in the woods or the mountains, familiar places that she wanted to visit again.

She had never been to the beach before.

She glanced around her, searching for Emma. She was there, still clasping her hand. A golden rope was wound around them.

"A true tether," Iris whispered, her eyebrows raising. She pulled at the knot, trying to see if it would come undone. It didn't. Even when she slipped her hand out of Emma's, the golden rope remained wound around their wrists, binding them together.

"What now?" Emma asked.

"Now, we find the person trying to kill us."

Emma nodded. She closed her eyes and her brow furrowed. As Iris watched, a thin, sputtering line bubbled on Emma's chest. It wavered for several seconds before completely snuffing out.

"What happened?" she asked.

Emma shook her head.

"I'm not sure," she admitted. "It's like something is blocking my ability. I can't—" She paused. "It's like someone knows I'm searching for them and doesn't want me to find them."

Iris cocked an eyebrow at her sister. "Has this ever happened to you before?"

"Never."

With the hand that wasn't bound to Emma, Iris ran her fingers through her hair. She didn't like the feeling that whoever had sent the golems to kill them had anticipated that they might search for them in the dreamworld. That meant they knew about both of their abilities.

"Okay," she said. "This is what we're going to do." She explained the outlines of a plan she'd formulated. Even as she was describing it, doubt began to settle in.

Emma gave her an incredulous look. "Do you really think this will work?"

Iris shrugged. "No idea. But what other option do we have?"

"Fair enough. Where do we begin?"

"Take my hands," Iris commanded.

They faced each other and clasped both hands. Iris smiled at her sister as she focused on finding the spell that blocked Emma from searching for the person.

She found it almost immediately. It was like a black aura hanging over Emma's head. She didn't want to think about how long it had been there—or who had placed it—but she quickly shattered the spell.

It seemed too easy, but she didn't know if that was because all the other spells she'd broken had been more complex, if she was growing in her abilities, or if this was a trap.

Part of her thought it was a trap.

She squeezed Emma's hands. She felt her sister's ability surge forward in a wave of heat and opened her eyes in time to see a beam of blue light erupt from Emma's chest and point towards the ocean.

She inclined her head towards the water. How could they possibly find a person in the sea?

"What now?" Emma asked, clearly confused by the direction her power was taking them.

Iris turned towards the ocean. If they had been in the real world, they would have needed to give up. Neither of them were strong swimmers. The only opportunities they'd had to swim had been in the river and creek beds, which were rarely deep enough for them to do more than wade in.

But they weren't in the real world.

Iris rubbed her hands together, the golden rope expanding to allow her range of motion. She imagined the seas parting, providing them a path forward. Her arms shook as she stretched them towards the water. There was a loud swooshing sound as the water slowly rose.

"What the void!" Emma shrieked as the ocean continued to well up, then divided in two.

Focused on keeping the water in place, Iris inched towards the walkway created by the divide. Sweat clung to her brow as she placed her first, tentative step onto the sea floor.

"How did you do this?" Emma asked. "Do you have an ability you haven't told me about yet? If you can do this—"

"I can only do this here because we're trapped in a dream, Emma. This isn't real."

"But I thought…" Emma trailed off.

"You thought we came here to destroy the models being used to control the golems?" Iris finished for her. "Yes, we are. I know this won't make sense. If I'm being honest, I still don't fully understand it, either, but here's the deal. The things we do here to other witches actually happen in the real world. We can die in here. We can hurt one another in here. And, we can break one another's spells."

"I still don't—"

"The golems are being controlled by a spell. We already know how to break it. We just need to find the mini versions of those monsters and shatter them."

Emma's look of confusion quickly shifted to determination as she stepped forward.

"Okay," she whispered. "If you think this is the way to defeat the rock monsters, let's do it."

They entered the pathway in silence. Giant fish shoved against the sea walls. Iris watched them with awe. She had never seen such beautiful and strange creatures before. One of the ones closer to the bottom of the water had fangs sticking out from its mouth and an antenna protruding from its forehead. None of them were able to leap from one side of the watery divide to the other. For that, Iris was grateful. She didn't want to think about what would happen if one of the fish landed on top of them.

Emma's blue light remained strong as they crept further and further into the ocean. The walls of water grew taller and the ocean floor sloped downward. There were places were giant cracks divided the ground, but Iris created bridges over them with a swipe of her hand. She smiled at how proficient she was becoming in manipulating the dreamworld.

Without warning, Emma's blue light began to waver. They shared a look, and then Iris focused on finding the spell that was blocking her sister's ability. Once again, she found a black aura blanketing Emma. This time, it took a little more concentration on her part to undo the spell. She had to spend several seconds tearing away the layers, but it eventually shattered.

A new doubt began to flood into her. What if this was a game? What if the mysterious strangers from before were simply luring them into the heart of the ocean just to collapse the walls and drown them both before Iris had an opportunity to wake them from the dreamworld.

She clenched her hands into fists and glanced at the ocean walls. They seemed secure, but she had no doubt that they would be able to crush both her and Emma if they came down. She debated revealing her concerns to Emma, but decided against it. If they didn't destroy the golems, it wasn't just their lives at stake. Micah and Chiara were also depending on them. Liam was, too.

So, Iris continued forward in silence.

The blue light led them to an underground city. Domes of shell and rock formed buildings. Each building was connected by what Iris could only describe as soap bubbles. It appeared abandoned.

"What is this place?" Emma asked as the shadow of the first structure blocked out the sister moons.

"I'm not sure," Iris admitted.

Emma placed her hand on one of the bubble-like tubes. Her hand passed through it and she stumbled. The golden rope tugged Iris, and they fell into the pathway.

The blue light emanating from Emma's chest extinguished in a puff of smoke. Iris immediately attempted to find the spell that had blocked her sister's ability, but when she searched for a spell, she found nothing. Frowning, she pushed to her feet. She was yanked downward since Emma didn't rise at the same time.

Footsteps echoed behind them. Iris spun around to find Elilda standing in the middle of the hallway. Her eyes gleamed red and her face was contorted with rage.

"You were supposed to save my coven," she hissed. "Not murder them in cold blood."

Emma stepped forward. "We didn't murder your coven sisters, you hag. They tried to kill us and defended ourselves. It's called self-defense."

"They would never—"

"They did," Iris interrupted. "They went against your direct command to track us. They poisoned Emma and nearly killed her in the process."

"I don't believe you." Elilda sniffed. "Why should I, Spellbreaker?"

Iris closed her eyes and breathed out heavily through her nose. It was back to this, then. She was really getting tired of this witch and her coven sisters blaming her for something she couldn't choose. It was not like she had a menu selection of powers and just decided to pick the one that put her in the most danger.

"You were the one who sent the golems?" Emma asked.

"Yes," Elilda replied. She stepped forward. A tiny statue of a golem poked out the top of her skirt pocket. She couldn't risk motioning to Emma to alert her of the golem.

She stepped forward, praying that the golden rope decided to expand this time and allow her full range of motion without dragging Emma too much.

"You made me a promise, Elilda," Iris said. "You told me none of your coven sisters would attack us or cause us harm. My sister almost died because what they did. I'm sorry we had to kill them. But you know what, I would do it again in a heartbeat if it meant that Emma and the rest of my friends were still alive to see another day."

Elilda scowled at her. "Bold words from a witch who's found herself in the middle of a spiderweb."

Iris laughed. "You don't scare me, Elilda. Not anymore." She took another step forward and the golden rope expanded. "You see, you made me realize something about myself when you sent me into that death trap. I am stronger than any of you, and that's why you're afraid of me. You're afraid that your petty, harsh spells will be"—she snapped her fingers—"crushed, just like that."

Elilda's lips parted slightly.

Iris continued to slowly advance towards her. "But what you failed to realize is that if you had just worked with me, taught me how to control my abilities, and helped me grow into the witch I know I'm going to be, you wouldn't have had to fear anything. I follow the Light, Elilda. Yours is the path of darkness."

Elilda pulled the golem doll from her pocket and held it before her like a lifeline. She hissed. "Take another step and I swear I'll order the golems to crush your little friends."

Iris paused. She hated that she couldn't see what was happening in the real world. Emma tugged on the golden rope, trying to draw her attention back to her, but Iris ignored it. Her sole focus was on Elilda and the doll.

"If you kill them, you won't have anything to leverage against me," Iris said. She kept her tone neutral.

Elilda laughed cruelly. "You have taken everything from me!"

"Who did we kill?" Emma asked, stepping forward. "She must have been someone very special to you."

Elilda's grip on the golem tightened as her gaze slid to Emma. She bared her teeth. "You want to know who you took from me? She was my whole world. Crinella." She whispered the name.

"She was my right-hand partner through the years. We have—had—been together for over one-hundred and fifty years." Tears streamed from her eyes. "She didn't agree with my decision to bargain with you so she took a band of our sisters to rid our world of the Spellbreaker. And you took her from me!"

Iris held up her hands, palms forward.

"I'm sorry," she whispered.

"Sorry? Oh, you're so sorry." Elilda laughed as she began pacing back and forth across the hallway. "That's rich coming from a Spellbreaker. You don't even understand what you've done. You just take and you take and you take and you never even try to make a change."

Iris took her chance and lunged for Elilda. Her head rammed into the witch's stomach, sending her careening backwards. She scrambled to get ahold of the golem doll, but Elilda kneed her in the chin.

She reeled backwards, dizziness swelling within her.

Emma was there in a heartbeat. She kicked Elilda in the stomach and then straddled her. With a ferocious cy, she wrapped her hands around the witch's neck and squeezed.

Iris, still dazed from being struck in the head, swayed forward. She blinked rapidly, trying to clear her vision. He gaze landed on the golem doll laying on the ground, several arms-lengths away from where Emma and Elilda were fighting.

She leapt for it. Her fingertips grazed it when she was suddenly jerked backwards by the golden rope tethering her to Emma. Her shoulder was wrenched out-of-socket as she was flung backwards. She slammed against the wooden door leading into one of the shell and stone buildings. Her head lolled to one side as she slid down the door and slumped to the ground.

"Iris?" Emma asked, shaking her. "Iris!"

Groaning, she looked up to see her sister hovering over her. Her cheeks were streaked and splotchy from crying and snot dripped from her nose.

"Gross," she said weakly, shoving Emma away.

Emma released a sigh of relief and sat back on her haunches. "Are you alright?"

"Just peachy," Iris responded more coldly than she intended. She tried moving her injured shoulder. Pain spread through her like wildfire. "I need you to pop my shoulder back into place," she whispered.

Emma shook her head.

"Do it," Iris commanded. "I can't fight her if you don't do this."

Emma nodded and, without warning, slipped Iris's shoulder forward. Iris screamed, and then relief flooded her.

There were soft cracks all around them as the remaining members of the Silver Skull coven materialized.

Iris had had enough. She'd risked her life to go after the people killing members of this coven. And, the only reason she'd killed any of them was because they had attacked her and the people she loved.

Clenching her fists, she rose to her feet. She steadied herself, then strode to the middle of the hallway, where Elilda ow stood, clutching the golem in one hand.

"You really want to do this?" Iris asked.

"You are an abomination. And you've only proven how untrustworthy you are by your actions. You didn't have to kill our sisters," Elilda said. Her face shifted to Emma. "How would you feel if someone killed your sister? Would you be willing to so easily forgive if those dead were people you loved above all others?"

"Yeah, like you've been trying to kill Iris this whole time?" Emma quipped.

Elilda's lips twitched. Iris looked down to see that she was manipulating the golem.

"No!" she screamed.

Light poured from her fingertips, her feet, her chest. She lifted from the ground as she focused on breaking the spell controlling the golem. All she could think about was saving Micah and Chiara from the golem. They'd come this far. She couldn't let the Silver Skull coven stop them now.

She cried as she felt her skin begin to disintegrate. She was being forced back into the real world against her will. Her body quaked from the effort of remaining in the dreamworld. She needed to finish this.

Stretching out her hands, she focused all her strength into a single, magical blow to the golem doll.

The last thing she saw was Elilda's look of rage as she was sucked back into her body.

Chapter Fifteen

Emma

Emma panted on the ground as she woke from the dream. She patted herself down, checking for any of the injuries she'd sustained while in the dreamworld. She found nothing, but she did feel weak, as if all the energy had been drained from her body. She groaned as she rolled over to check on Iris.

A giant fist slammed into the ground right next to her head. She screamed.

She looked up as the golem slowly crumbled into pieces. The hand next to her uncurled, its fat fingers splaying.

"Are you alright?" she asked, cradling her sister to her chest.

Iris pushed away from her and glanced around the encampment.

"Where are Micah and Chiara?" she asked, her voice tight.

Emma suddenly felt cold. She hadn't checked for them. She scanned the area but didn't see any signs of them. The camp was full of cracked boulders. The horses were gone and so were their friends.

She rose to her feet and stormed around the camp, calling their names. No response came.

Panic swelled within her and she began shoving rocks to the side, praying to the Light that they hadn't been crushed when the golem broke.

"Where are they?" Iris cried. She still sat on the ground, clearly too stunned to do much else.

Emma didn't have an answer.

She pushed against a large rock. Her muscles strained and sweat dripped from her brow. Underneath, remnants of bones and flesh with puddles of blood.

"No," she whispered, then shoved more of the rocks aside. "No, no, no!"

Tears blurred her vision.

Iris approached her and wrapped her arms around her shoulders and pulled her into a tight embrace.

"Who was it?" she whispered.

Emma shook her head.

Iris ambled over to the overturned another boulder and looked down. Her cheeks paled and, when she looked back at Emma, tears were streaming down her cheeks.

"It's one of the horses," she said. "It's just one of the horses."

Relief swelled within Emma that it wasn't one of her friends, but also sorrow for the loss of their horse. Her heart rammed against her chest as anxiety filled her. If one of their horses could be crushed to death like this, what had happened to Chiara and Micah?

She scrambled to her feet and began recklessly rolling rocks over. Each time she dislodged a large one, she prayed she wouldn't find them crushed beneath it.

"They can't have just disappeared," Iris said. She sank to the ground. Her face was covered in dust and grime. Her hair was matted and knotted.

Emma tugged on one of her braids as she contemplated what to do next. They had no horses. No supplies. Everything had been destroyed by the golems. And, to make matters worse, they couldn't find their friends.

"Is there a chance we just didn't find them in the rubble?" she asked.

Iris shook her head. "We've been searching for hours and haven't been able to find them, Emma. Do you really think they're still here?"

Emma scanned the debris one last time. "They must have ran away when—"

"They wouldn't have abandoned us," Iris cut in. "You know that."

To be fair, Emma didn't know that. She trusted Chiara, but she also knew her friend had a deep sense of self-preservation.

"We have to find them," Iris muttered, more to herself than to Emma.

Closing her eyes, Emma breathed in deeply. She felt the way the air filled her lungs. She forced her breath down as deep as it would go and keep inhaling. Her lungs filled bit by bit until she though they couldn't expand anymore. She held it there for several seconds, just feeling the weight of her own breath in her chest. Knowing that she was alive. That she had a purpose.

And then she exhaled just as slowly. Her chest deflated, her shoulders sagging as the tension she'd been holding released.

"We'll track them," she said.

Iris looked at her. Her eyes were full of tears and her nose was red from wiping it on the hem of her sleeve.

"Did you hear me?" Emma asked. "I've been doing this my entire life, Iris. I'm even more efficient now that I have the ability to find lost things." She reached over and tucked a lock of Iris's hair behind her ear. "We'll find them. And then, we'll rescue Liam."

Wordlessly, Iris nodded. Her eyes were puffy and pink from crying, but there was a look of determination in her eyes as she leaned in to embrace Emma.

Emma stroked her sister's back and prayed that she hadn't just given her false hope.

She was strong.

She was a huntress.

But she was also terrified of what they might discover once they found their friends.

After a moment, she gently extracted herself from Iris's grasp and began to walk the perimeter of the camp. Overturned boulders had knocked into trees and covered the ground with debris. She found it difficult to make heads or tails of the destruction.

At one point, she thought she saw footprints in the dirt, but then realized they belonged to Iris and herself. She frowned. There had to be something to show her what had happened here while they were in the dreamworld.

She was just beginning to lose hope of finding a single clue when she noticed a bit of white lace on the forest floor, close to where the golems had entered their camp. It was way too fine for anything she or Iris would wear. But then, she spotted another little sliver of lace by one of the trees further down the path they'd assumed was just the entrance the golems had taken into the camp.

She walked over to the second piece, then fell to her knees as she picked it up and cradled it to her chest.

"Thank you," she whispered as she looked further down the path and saw more bits of lace. She couldn't explain it, but she knew Chiara had left the lace for her to find.

"Iris!" she called and motioned for her sister to join her. She bent closer over the tracks, trailing her fingers over the ridges, and realized something she'd missed earlier.

There were footprints leading into but also out of the camp.

Iris came up beside her. She didn't say anything as she handed Iris the bit of lace and pointed down the golem-made path. Iris sighed in relief and squeezed her sister's shoulder, then she moved down the path, her eyes glued to the ground. They searched for more signs as to where the golems had taken their friends.

Eventually the lace ran out and transitioned into strips of cotton. Emma picked each one up and examined the ground around where she'd found it. Nothing led her to believe that the golems had taken them off the path.

Eventually, they came to a fork in the trail. Emma walked down each side for several paces but didn't find a single bit of lace or any strips of cloth in either direction. She didn't know if Chiara and Micah had simply run out of things to drop or if the golems had done something to them.

"Any clue which way they took them?" Iris asked as she came up beside Emma.

"None," Emma replied.

"Can you use your ability to seek them out?"

Emma shook her head. Nothing happened. She didn't know if whatever curse the coven had placed on her was still in effect or if—she couldn't even bring herself to think about what if.

Iris placed both hands on either side of Emma's face and breathed in deeply. Her body vibrated and beads of sweat slid down her brow. After a moment, she pulled away, panting hard.

"Try again," she said in a shaky voice.

Emma closed her eyes and envisioned hearing Micah's laugh. He didn't laugh very often, but when he did, it was warm and loud and made her feel giddy inside just hearing it. A smile touched her lips as she remembered how he cradled her to his chest when she was injured. How he had been patient with her all those months she refused to say even two words to him. How, even now, when she was still rude to him sometimes, he took it in stride.

She felt warm and fuzzy all over.

When she opened her eyes, a golden line of light streamed from her chest.

"That's new," she whispered as she began walking in the direction it pointed, gripping the pieces of cloth they had found.

They moved at a slow pace. Emma wanted to go faster, but every time she increased the tempo, Iris fell farther behind. Emma wondered how much of her strength she used each time she broke one of the spells.

They rounded a corner, and Emma scanned the ground for any clues.

To her left, Iris fell to the ground with a thud, skinning her knees.

"Let's take a break," Emma whispered.

They needed to find Micah and Chiara, but Iris had already overextended herself.

Iris shook her head. "We can't stop here," she said.

She sighed softly as she sat back and eased the small rocks out of her flesh.

Emma came over and bandaged the wounds with one of the strips of cloth. It wasn't the most sanitary of bindings, but it would do until they found more resources.

"How much further do you think they took them?" Iris asked.

"Honestly, I'm not sure," Emma replied. She didn't add that she was worried the golems may have separated their friends. She prayed that her power wasn't failing or tricking her. That they were actually following the correct path to Micah.

But what about Chiara? She was afraid to switch her focus lest she lose sight of Micah.

"We have to keep moving," Iris said as she pushed herself up. She wobbled as she took a step forward.

"Whoa, there," Emma said, placing a steadying hand on Iris's back. "We can continue going nice and slow."

Iris ducked her head, a deep blush forming on her cheeks. Emma didn't understand her sister sometimes. She was clearly fatigued and injured. There was no reason not to go slowly.

She was about to say as much when shouting erupted from in front of them.

Chapter Sixteen

Emma

Emma charged forward. She didn't care that she only had the four daggers strapped to her body as weapons. She didn't care that she left Iris behind as she sprinted forward. Those shouts could belong to anyone, but something within her knew that they belonged to Micah.

The golden line of light grew brighter as she raced through the trees. She barely noticed how the path cleared by the golems grew smaller and narrower the farther along it went. Eventually, the path ran out altogether. She dropped to her knees, searching for any clue as to what had happened. Giant rock monsters didn't just disappear into thin air with a snap of the fingers. Besides, her light was guiding her to Micah.

He had to be there. Somewhere.

At least, she hoped he was.

More shouts joined the first.

Leaping to her feet, she followed the sound. Grinding stone met her as she rounded a corner. She skidded to a halt just as a chunk of rock landed in front of her. She didn't waste any time. She bounded over the stone and into the fray.

Her jaw dropped when she discovered what was happening. A band of elves formed a circle around Micah and Chiara's limp bodies. They formed two rings. The inner ring had their eyes closed and were clearly casting spells. The outer ring shot arrows at the rock monsters, which were attempting to break through the outer ring of elves.

Emma cocked her head. There was no way the arrows would be strong enough to pierce rock. They would just glance off, more an annoyance than anything else.

Five golems surrounded her friends and the elves. Each time they drew in closer, one of the magic-wielding elves launched a volley of molten lava at the beasts. Rock melted in a matter of seconds when it struck them. Bits of the golems were strewn across the field. But still, they continued to fight against the elves.

Emma wove her way between their legs and charged across the field. She prayed the elves wouldn't shoot her as she drew closer. They barely seemed to notice her at all as they continued attacking the golems. The golden light from her chest formed an aura all around her as she slipped through the outer ring of elves.

A firm hand clasped her shoulder.

"What's your name, girl?" a man asked.

She shoved against his hand and peeked her head through a gap in the inner circle.

"What is she doing here?" one of the men asked, looking Emma up and down for a moment.

"She's the Starseeker," one of the elves whispered.

"Let her through," said another.

The elf with his hand on her shoulder quickly withdrew it.

"Sorry, mistress Valka," he whispered.

S.A. McClure

She looked up at him, blinking. "How do you know my name?"

"We have a Keeper with us," one of them responded.

Emma had absolutely no idea what they were talking about, but she was thankful they'd let her through. She squatted across from Micah and Chiara. Their breathing was steady, but each had an array of wounds that looked like they'd been left to suffer thorough.

She reached out a hand and traced the curves of Micah's face as he slept. The warm feeling in her gut expanded. She sighed, relieved that they were alright.

"What can I do to help?" she asked.

"Are you good with a bow?" one of the elves from the outer circle asked.

She almost laughed at the question. She slid through a gap in the inner circle and held out her hand to the elf who was talking to her.

"Name's Emmaleigh, but you can call me Em or Emma. You're choice. I've been training for this my whole life."

"Okay," the elf said, "That's a little weird."

Emma chuckled. She was a little weird.

"There's a chest on the ground, open it and find the toy bow inside," the elf instructed.

"You're seriously going to give me a toy bow?" she asked. She glanced down at a large, wooden chest on the ground. *What an insult*, she thought as she lifted the chest's lid and scrounged around inside until she found a miniature bow, complete with little jewels and hardened leather protecting the joints.

She pulled back on the string to test how firm it was when the bow suddenly began to tremble in her hands. It grew in size until it was a full-size bow, just like the ones on the outer ring were using. A quiver of arrows appeared on her back.

"How in the—"

"Never mind that," the elf said. He stepped to the left, creating a small hole in their defenses.

Emma stepped up to the plate and drew her first arrow. Her muscles strained against the motion, but she savored the sensation. She'd missed this.

She smiled a little as she released her first volley and it struck the golem squarely in the head. Instead of glancing off the way she had anticipated, it burned a hole in the golem's head, melting the rock and turning it into lava. Her eyes grew wide as the golem swatted at its head, trying to extinguish the flame. Its hands melted but it was successful.

"Nice shot," the elf said from beside her. "My name is Eldridge, by the way."

She snorted. "What kind of a name is Eldridge?" she asked, scrunching her nose at the thought having to say that name all the time.

"Are you seriously mocking my name in the middle of a battle?" he asked.

"Why not?" she retorted as she launched another arrow. "It seems like the perfect time to lighten the mood."

"Humans really are a strange species."

"Right, well, thank you for that," she murmured as she released another arrow at one of the golems. It struck where its right arm connected to the rest of its body. The joint turned to molten lava as the arm slid away.

The golem stumbled, clearly off-balance from just losing its arm. Emma smirked and glanced at Eldridge. He concentrated on his aim and released one arrow at the same golem's head, quickly fired another one that struck its left side, and then shot a third that struck the left knee.

The golem began melting at a rapid pace. It swayed as its left leg fell away and then collapsed to the ground in a heap.

Emma gave a whoop of joy.

A stream of lava shot over her head and knocked one of the golems to the ground. It roared and pounded at the earth, shaking them. More of its companions began to do the same, creating an earthquake all around them.

Her feet slipped over crumbling ground. She leapt backwards and slammed into one of the magic-wielding elves.

"Sorry," she mumbled as she ducked beneath the elf's outstretched arm and rushed to where Chiara and Micah both lay on the ground.

The golems began pounding on the ground in unison. More cracks appeared. Emma dropped to the ground and looped her arm around Micah's neck and held on tightly as the ground shifted beneath them. She wrapped her legs around Chiara. She didn't know how long she would be able to hold onto them if the ground beneath them completely gave out, but she hoped they'd be able to survive whatever fall was in store for them.

The elves suddenly stopped firing at the golems. Instead, they laid their bows down and began chanting in a tongue Emma didn't recognize.

Thousands of starbugs fluttered into the clearing. They glowed brilliantly, casting out all shadows.

One of the elves from in the inner ring stepped forward, her arms outstretched and her face serene.

She sang, her voice rising and falling in a melody that pulled at the back of Emma's memory. It was eerily beautiful and sad all at the same time.

A loud boom reverberated across the clearly. Everything happened so quickly: Emma's ears rang and her head whipped backwards at the explosion. The starbugs burst into a plume of smoke and shimmering light. A translucent dome formed all around them as boulders, dust, and rubble clattered on top of them.

The dome protected them from being smashed to bits.

Emma clutched onto Micah as one rock landed directly above her. She cringed as it harmlessly rolled down the side of the dome and thudded to the ground.

Her chest tightened.

Iris was still out there. She hadn't been with them. She could be hurt.

Emma began breathing rapidly and shallowly. Her mind hazed from the lack of oxygen reaching her brain. Tears stung her eyes and it was all she could do to continue holding onto Micah and Chiara as the last of the golems exploded.

She leapt to her feet. Dust sparkled as it caught moonlight. It coated everything. She coughed as she stepped beyond the magical barrier. Rubble shifted under her feet as she slowly made her way across the clearing. Her eyes stung from the debris landing in them.

"Iris!" she called.

No response.

Frantically, she shoved aside larger boulders and tried to determine the best path across the field. She tripped as one of the rocks rolled beneath her feet, twisting her ankle. She grunted in pain, but forced herself to apply weight to the injured leg as she continued looking for her sister.

Something shifted to her left. She spun towards the sound. Hope swelled within her. She'd thought she'd lost Micah and Chiara today. They had been fine. There was no reason to assume that Iris would be any different. She'd been further away from the fight, anyway. The trees should have provided a modicum of protection.

More rocks shifted under her feet and she stumbled forward, falling on her knees. A jagged piece of rock punctured her leg, right below her kneecap. She screamed. The jagged rock remained wedged in her leg as she stood.

"Iris!" she called again, her voice breaking. She couldn't find her. She attempted taking a step forward, but her now twice injured leg collapsed beneath her weight.

Eldridge glided over the rubble as if it were a smooth cobblestone road. He stooped to examine her leg and made a tsking.

"You're going to be alright," he said as he laid a cool hand on her forehead. She didn't have to time react as her entire body became numb. He pulled a water skin from his belt and uncorked it. Using two fingers, he pried her lips open and poured some of the contents down her throat.

It tasted like burnt gizzards and moldy cheese. She choked and he closed her lips until she swallowed all the contents. He released her mouth, then examined her injuries again. There was a loud squelching noise as he pulled the rock from her leg. Strangely, she didn't feel the pain.

He leaned over her legs and began doing something. Emma could not tell what since she couldn't feel anything. She tried to ask, but her lips wouldn't cooperate with her brain. Panic made her heart hammer in her chest and her mind go hazy as she continued to try moving.

A few moments passed in silence and then Eldridge leaned over and said, "It'll itch over the next several days, but you will walk again."

Although she didn't know if the muscles around her eyes responded to her, she imagined glaring at him. A few more elves leaned over her, inspecting her for additional wounds. They placed smelly ointments on her cuts and bruises and made tsking sounds each time they discovered a new, untreated injury.

All Emma could think about was where Iris was. While she was being treated for relatively minor injuries, her sister could be being crushed by the weight of stone. Or slowly suffocating. Or lying broken at the bottom of one of the deep ravines caused by the golems' pounding fists.

"Everything will be alright," Eldridge said, placing his hand on her forehead again. A wisp of warm passed from him to her and she blinked at him in surprise.

"My sister?" she asked. To her surprise, words actually came out of her mouth this time.

"With our healer," he said with a smile. "I know this all must be shock to you."

That was the understatement of the year. Not very many elves chose to live in Dramadoon. Most stayed in the Encartia, home of the elves.

"What are you doing here?" she asked.

"We are here as envoys of the King," he replied.

"Dramadoon doesn't have a king," she said.

He laughed. "No, she does not."

Emma cocked her head towards him and asked again, "What is your purpose in coming here?"

He sighed. "There is a darkness to the west. Strange things have happened. The Princess is missing. Most believe her to be dead. The King does not."

Emma shook her head. "Which king?"

"Colin of Szarmi," Eldridge replied without missing a beat. "King of Szarmi."

"Can you call yourself that if you don't have the throne?"

"He will."

"You seem rather confident in him," she said. "I thought elves and Szarmians were mortal enemies."

He gave her a half-smile. "They used to be. Some believe they still are." He shrugged. "Regardless, we are here seeking aid from the Prince and Princess of Dramadoon."

She blinked at him. First Chiara was talking about war and now this. She chewed on her bottom lip as she contemplated his words. She didn't know how everything fit together, but she was beginning to wonder if there was something much bigger and darker happening in the world beyond their little sphere. She shook her head. She could consider that later. For now, all she wanted was to make sure her sister was well.

"I want to see Iris," she said.

He pointed to a row of tents set up just beyond the rubble and pointed.

"She's over there," he said.

As she went, Eldridge called after her, "You cannot ignore the darkness forever. Eventually, it will consume everything, leaving us to wander alone in streets filled with broken dreams. We could use a fighter like you in the pending battle."

Her back stiffened at his words. The farther they traveled from home, the more she realized she wished they'd never left.

Chapter Seventeen

Emma

The heat was oppressive as Emma crouched behind the bushes. It rained that morning and the scent of damp earth and wild animals clung to the air. She breathed in deeply, letting it remind her of home. Birds chirped as they hopped from branch to branch, singing to one another.

She inhaled as she spotted the white tail and brown fur of the deer. It bent its head to munch on a bush of berries. Exhaling, she released her arrow with a low ping.

Birds scattered at the sound. Other deer ran. But the one she'd been aiming at fell to the ground, an arrow protruding from its eye. She smiled as she stood. She set about tying the deer to a sturdy looking branch she found in the woods. She could already taste the venison stew she intended to make with the deer tonight.

"Emmaleigh." Eldridge's voice came from behind her.

She jumped and turned to face him.

"How do you do that?" she asked, her voice pitched.

"Do what?" he asked.

"Sneak up on me like that without making a sound. I mean, I know how to be quiet in the forest, but you… you make it seem easy."

He shrugged. "When you have lived as long as I have and your sole means of survival was based on being stealthy, it changes how you interact with your environment."

She gave him a puzzled look, but decided to move past his vague comments.

"What do you want?" she asked.

Better to get straight to the point. Over the past two days, he'd reiterated his interest in having her join their group of fighters. He considered her a valuable asset, after seeing how she handled the flaming blow.

"We leave at first light tomorrow, Emmaleigh. My brethren and I have discussed it at length. We would be honored if you would join us."

"I can't," she said. "My place is with my sister."

"The healer," he mused, rubbing his jaw. "Yes, we've invited her to join us as well."

Emma rolled her eyes at him. "Let me guess, she declined you outright and told you never to ask again."

He chuckled at her, "It did go something like that."

"Of course it did. She's void-bent on finding someone."

"She may have mentioned that in her long reasoning for why she couldn't join us," he said. "But I fail to see why you have to make the same choice."

Emma shook her head. "Iris is all I have in the world. She and I have been through so much together. I can't abandon her now. She wants to find him, and I want to keep her safe. I want her to be happy."

He helped her lift the deer by taking the back half of the makeshift pole. "You are not your sister, Emma. There is a fighting spirit within you."

"You don't know Iris," she said with a smile. She used to think her sister was weak. Somewhere along the way, that had changed. She now knew that Iris was stronger than anyone realized, especially herself.

"Is there nothing that could convince you to join us?"

She inhaled deeply at the question. She wanted the adventure and comradery she knew going with him would mean. Her heart told her to tell him that she wanted to join him more than anything, that she was willing to leave Iris to fight with them. But her head squashed the words before they had time to leap from her lips.

"Until we find Liam, I am with Iris," she said, hedging her response.

"I see."

They traveled in silence for several moments, hauling the deer between them.

"I will respect your wishes, Emmaleigh Valka, Starseeker."

"You don't have to call me that," she said.

"Those who seek the light in the darkness are treasured among my people," Eldridge said with a shrug. "Your ability is one that is always searching for the light, even in the darkest of hours."

She rolled her eyes, even though he couldn't see her face. "My sister has the better abilities," she said. "She's stronger than I can ever hope to be."

"Your sister does have great strength," he agreed, "but her ability to break other witch's spells is a dark smear upon her name."

Emma almost released her half of the pole at the anger in his tone. She didn't understand how anyone with magic could promote the killing of innocents simply for having a certain ability. Wasn't that the same as the Szarmians killing magicals in the first place? She ground her teeth. She was tired of her sister being treated like a second-class citizen for something she didn't have any control over. It's not like Iris chose to have this ability. It was gifted to her by the Light.

"I can sense your anger," Eldridge said.

Emma dropped the deer and turned to face him. She jabbed him in the chest with her pointer finger. "You may think that Iris will turn to Darkness, and you know what, maybe she will. But I can promise you one thing, it won't be because she was weak or misguided. It won't even be because the Darkness seduced her. You want to know why my sister would ever, in a million years, decide to use her abilities for ill? It would be because people like you pushed her that way!"

She turned to leave, but Eldridge grasped her wrist.

"How can you say such things? We are not hurting her. We are not tempting her!"

"No, you're not. But you are making her feel isolated. All Iris wants to do is heal people and do good in this world. That's it. But every time she meets someone new and they find out she has the ability to break their spells or block their magical abilities, they treat her like last week's garbage. So, forgive me for saying that what you're doing is worse than anything she could ever do." She stomped her foot. "And, if you want my opinion, treating her like this without taking the time to get to know her makes you a hypocrite."

He blinked at her and remained silent for several moments.

"I am sorry if I have offended you," he said at length.

"Don't apologize to me," she hissed. "Apologize to Iris!"

She struggled against his hold on her wrist. When she couldn't break it, she shot him a glare she hoped he understood. His grip loosened and he stared down at his hands for several moments.

"I will think on your words," he said stiltedly. He bent to pick up his end of the pole. He nodded towards her end. "Shall we?"

She scowled at him. She couldn't force him to change his mind anymore than she could strip Iris of her powers. And she wouldn't want to, either. It would mean more if he came to the realization of his own accord.

She picked up the stick and set as fast a pace as she could back to their small. She didn't speak to him once the entire way there and, thankfully, he didn't attempt to engage her in any further conversation either.

Emma rose before dawn. She checked on Micah, who was in his bedroll, first. His hair was tousled, and a bit of drool was running down his chin. She smiled at him and wondered what he would have done if he'd never been sent to spy on them. To hunt them.

Of course, he'd broken the rules by protecting them.

She considered if he even knew why he'd done it.

A memory floated to the forefront of her mind. It was winter again and she was standing in Grandmother Rel's cottage as something pounded on the door. A giant, inky blob stormed into the room and attacked her. A wolf—Liam—saved her. He was wounded. Bleeding. She turned back to help him because he'd helped her.

Tears stung her eyes. He'd been protecting her ever since.

She leaned down and smoothed his hair back from his face. His eyelids fluttered. She wished she knew what he was dreaming about. He looked so peaceful.

She shook her head. There wasn't time for her to consider her changing feelings for him. They still needed to find Liam and she needed to decide what she was going to do after they did.

She went to check on Chiara next, but her bedroll was missing. Emma ran outside, already knowing what was happening.

Chiara was tying the new pack the elves had given her to a fresh horse. Emma wasn't sure where they'd procured the horses, but she was thankful they had. They brought enough for everyone to have a mount in the coming days, including Micah, Iris, Chiara, and herself.

She hurried over to Chiara.

"You're leaving?" she asked, placing her hand on Chiara's saddle.

"I have to," she whispered. "I told you before, I want to join the fight. My powers may be of use."

Emma nodded. She understood her friend's desire to be useful.

"You could come with us," Chiara whispered. "Micah could continue the journey with Iris. You don't need—"

Emma shook her head. "I can't leave her," she said. "Not yet. I promised her I would be with her until the end. And I intend to keep that promise."

Chiara nodded, her lips pressed together.

After a silent pause, Emma leaned forward and they embraced one another tightly.

"Keep me posted on your whereabouts," Emma said. "I want to know everything."

"I promise," Chiara said, voice hoard.

"Ahem."

They both spun around to Eldridge standing behind them. Emma glared at him, and Chiara smiled.

"What do you want, Eldridge?" Emma asked.

He bowed to her and then held out a package wrapped in brown paper. It was tied up with a bow on top and everything.

"What is this?" Emma asked with a scowl as she accepted the package.

He shrugged. "Perhaps, in the future, you will decide to join our riders."

She untied the string and pulled back the paper to find the miniature bow she'd used during the fight against the golems, a small jar of shimmering dust, and a dagger with an onyx blade. She glanced up at him, confused.

"My brethren and I decided that you should have the tools every one of us has," he said. "With this bow, you can carry it with you wherever you go." He snatched it from her hand and pulled back on the string. It grew to full-size, just as it had during the battle with the golems. He then pressed on a ruby set in the handle riser. The bow shimmered slightly before condensing back into its miniature form.

Emma nodded and held her hand out to take the bow back.

"Thank you," she said. "But what are these other things for?" She motioned towards the rest of the items.

He picked up the jar of sparkling dust. "I told you before that you strike me as someone who always seeks the Light. This dust will help you light up the world. Use is sparingly, as there is a limited quantity left."

"How is dust supposed to help me light up the world?" she asked, crossing her arms over her chest.

"Blow a scoop of this dust into the air and follow it. Like the starbugs, it will glow. I hope it bring you comfort in the days to come. The Darkness is stirring and will be here soon."

She shot him an agitated glance, but motioned for him to continue.

He picked up the blade. "This dagger strips any who are killed by it of their eternal essence."

Emma's jaw dropped and she took a step back. "I don't want to do that to anyone," she said. "You can keep it."

He shook his head. "The Light intended for us to rid the world of evil using it. We trust you to know the difference between those who do dark things and those who have dark souls."

She stared at him, perplexed. He shoved the dagger towards her.

She shook her head. "I still don't want it."

"If you don't take it, then I will," Chiara said, reaching out for it.

Sighing, Emma snatched it before Chiara could. She didn't know what made her change her mind. It wasn't exactly that she didn't want Chiara to have it, but something about the dagger called to her. She stared down at the onyx blade. It glittered like the stars in the first rays of sunshine.

Eldridge placed both hands on her shoulders and smiled. "I know one day we will meet again," he said. "I pray that day is soon."

He kissed her on her brow and turned away.

Chiara and Emma shared a look and laughed when they thought he was out of earshot.

"He really is the most pretentious person—sorry, elf—I think I've ever met," Emma said.

"Yes, but he seems to have a soft spot for you."

Emma sobered and shook her head. "It's not like that."

"I'm sorry," Chiara said quickly. "I didn't mean it."

Emma shrugged. "It's fine."

The elves loaded their packs onto horses. Emma knew they would leave soon. Her chest tightened and she wrapped her arms around Chiara again.

"I hope to see you again," Chiara murmured.

Her tears soaked the top of Emma's blouse. Other than her sister, Chiara had been her first true female friend. Sure, she'd gotten along with the animals-turned-human Iris had saved from Balkeen, but Chiara had been the first person Emma had related to on a different level. She felt comfortable around her. She could be herself.

"I'll miss you," Emma whispered.

"And I, you."

They held each for another moment. Emma breathed in her scent. She smelled like woodsmoke and cherries.

A smile spread across her face as she pulled back and said, "The next time we see each other, I expect you to create a raging purple fire for me. We can roast a pig or something over it."

Chiara laughed. "That would be nice, wouldn't it?"

They hugged one more time and then Eldridge and the rest of the elves began riding away.

"Go," Emma whispered, extracting herself from Chiara's grasp.

Chiara ducked her head and mounted her horse. With a glance back at Emma, she nudged the horse forward.

Emma clutched the three items from Eldridge to her chest as she watched Chiara ride away, joining with the elves headed into battle. She wished she could be among them. Maybe one day she would be. That is, if she survived another encounter with Grandmother Rel.

Chapter Eighteen

Iris

Iris jolted awake. Her head pounded and she leaned over the edge of her bedroll and threw up. She wiped the bile from her lips with the back of her hand and stood. Her entire body quivered.

She knew where Liam was.

She coughed as more bile filled her mouth and her stomach clenched.

She knew everything Grandmother Rel had done to him.

Closing her eyes, she breathed in deeply. Her stomach ached and fluttered with anxiety. They had no time to lose.

Grandmother Rel hadn't been kidding when she'd given Iris the threat: come get him or else. Well, the 'or else' was happening and Iris couldn't stand by and let it continue.

She stumbled out of her small tent and wandered over to Emma's. Peeping her head in, she realized her sister wasn't there. She straightened, the movement sending her stomach into a frenzied clenching sequence again. She swayed and nearly vomited all over the entrance to Emma's tent.

"Are you alright?" Emma asked from behind her, laying a cool hand on her back. Although it was early morning, it was already sweltering.

Iris fanned herself with her hands as she turned and met Emma's gaze. Her legs wobbled.

"There's no time to waste," she said as she collapsed into Emma's arms.

Emma stroked her back as she held her. "You smell like the rotting side of a fish."

"I'm sorry," Iris wailed.

Emma guided her to the ground and sat, cross-legged in front of her. For the first time, Iris noticed that Emma was carrying a small dagger, a jar of sparkling dust, and a miniature bow in her hands.

"Gifts from the elves?" she asked, gesturing towards the items.

Emma nodded. "They rode out this morning. Chiara with them."

Iris formed a small 'o' with her lips and stared down at her hands. She was sad she didn't get a chance to say goodbye to Chiara. It was strange that she would slip away without telling her. They had been friends, hadn't they? She chewed on her bottom lip. Or did Chiara share the others' opinions that she was too dangerous? A freak? An abomination?

She sighed heavily and met Emma's gaze again. Tears caught on her eyelashes, making it difficult to see.

Emma grasped her hand.

"I'm sorry she didn't say goodbye," she whispered.

Iris shrugged and forced herself to look at the items the elves had given her sister.

"What do they all do?" she asked, genuinely curious.

A small smile tugged at Emma's lips. "Well, this one," she said, touching the jar of dust, "glows when you blow on it."

Iris laughed. "Is that all?"

Emma shrugged. "That's all Eldridge told me."

"Alright," she replied dubiously, "what about the rest of the items?"

"The dagger strips the other person of their essence."

Iris gasped. "You can't use that! That's not what the Light intends for us to do, Emma. Not ever."

"I know," she replied, a tad on the defensive side. "I didn't want to accept it, but Chiara and Eldridge made me." She sheathed the dagger and slipped it into her boot. "I promise I'll never use it."

"You better not." Iris ran her tongue along her upper teeth, wishing for a glass of water.

Emma nodded once and then continued. "The bow is my favorite one. Watch this."

As she pulled back on the string, it grew to be the proper size.

"Okay. I'll give it to Eldridge. That one is pretty amazing," Iris said.

A wave of lightheadedness caught her. She keeled forward, her hands barely catching her head before she face-planted into the ground.

"Iris!" Emma wrapped her arms around her and pulled in tight. "What's wrong?"

The sun was too bright on her eyes. It made her head feel like it could explode at any moment.

Closing her eyes, she snuggled against her sister and whispered, "I know where Liam is."

"What! How?"

"Grandmother Rel met me in the dreamworld. I don't know how she got there. She told me she'd be willing to make a bargain with me for Liam's life. And then she gave me directions."

"Uh, Iris, I know how much you want to rescue Liam, but do you really think that's a good idea? This sounds like a trap, if you ask me."

"I don't care!" Iris snapped. She immediately wished she hadn't. "I'm sorry, Emma."

Emma squeezed her tightly and said, "Tell me more about what happened."

"I didn't intend to go to the dreamworld this time. It keeps getting more and more difficult to avoid when I fall asleep. I can't escape it, even when I want to." She brushed away hot tears as they trailed down her cheeks. "I didn't want to tell you because I knew you'd say it was a trap."

They stared at each other for a moment.

"Alright, yes. I know," Emma said. "That's exactly how I reacted, but you have to understand. Doesn't it seem a little strange to you that you suddenly discover Grandmother Rel in the dreamworld without even trying and then she mysteriously tells you exactly where to find her?"

Iris bobbed her head at Emma's words. Part of her knew her sister was right. It was the reason she'd hesitated in saying anything at all.

"It does seem a bit strange," she conceded.

"A bit?" Emma replied incredulously. "Come on, Iris. You are smarter than this!"

Iris leaned back, creating enough space between them that she could peer into Emma's eyes. "I know you think I'm being irrational—"

"Because you are!"

"But I think you need to consider the fact that I love him, Emma." It was the first time she'd said it so straightforwardly and she immediately felt awkward. How could she be in love with someone she barely knew? They'd met in the dreamworld several times, but he was still a mystery to her. Almost a stranger.

Emma's nostrils flared. Iris had never seen her sister with such consternation on her face before. Not even when she'd argued with Grandmother Rel. A small vein in her neck twitched as she glared at Iris.

"I know you care about him, Iris," she said through gritted teeth, "but he is not the one for you. What do you even know about him? Really?"

"I'm not having this conversation with you."

Emma's eyebrows rose.

Iris inhaled deeply before forcing herself to stand. She swayed, her head still pounding.

"I get it. You want to go save the world. So, do it. I don't need you," she said. "I know where to go now." Tears sprang to her eyes as she spoke, but she continued anyway. "I want you to go." She didn't. But, she also didn't want to be the reason Emma stayed.

Silence hung between them.

"You don't mean that," Emma said.

"I do."

Iris turned away as the tears began to flow down her cheeks. She stormed back into her tent and began throwing items into her pack. She wanted Emma to come after her. To tell her that she was sorry. To allow her to apologize, too.

But she knew it wasn't going to happen. They rarely argued, and never like what had just occurred.

She chewed on her bottom lip, contemplating whether she should be the first to say something. Part of her wanted to, but another, stronger part wanted to wait for Emma to be the one to breakdown first.

The sun rose higher in the sky. If she didn't leave soon, she'd lose too much of the day. She sighed. She didn't want to argue with Emma.

She ducked out of her tent, intending to find Emma and hash it out. They were both under a lot of stress. In the end, they needed to stick together.

She halted. Her sister's tent was gone. As was the horse the elves had given her.

She was alone.

"No," she whispered. "Emma!" she called as she stumbled towards the tree line. She called her sister's name over and over again as she searched for her.

No response.

"Emma!" she screamed.

Still nothing.

She'd really done it. She'd left. She was gone.

Iris sank to the ground and sobbed.

Chapter Nineteen

Iris

Iris took the rest of the day to rest. After the time she'd spent searching for Emma and sobbing, alone in the forest, she didn't have the inclination to start the final leg of her quest to find Liam.

She felt numb.

Micah had gone as well. They'd abandoned her when they had been so close to their destination. She was less than a day's ride from where Grandmother Rel was holding Liam.

If they had just stayed—she stopped herself from going down that path. It was no use. They'd made their decision and she had made hers. She'd committed herself to rescuing Liam. And that was exactly what she was going to do.

She half-expected to wake up the following morning to find that Emma had thought better of leaving her. To see her sitting at a fire cooking breakfast or carrying in a rabbit to smoke for a bit before continuing their journey.

But what she got instead was an empty, cold camp. No one had come back for her.

Iris packed quickly and rode hard towards the location Grandmother Rel had indicated on the map she'd shown her in the dreamworld. She barely stopped to eat or to pee. After several hours in oppressive late summer heat, her horse began foaming at the mouth. She knew she needed to give her a rest, but everything within her was coiled and ready to spring to action.

"I'm sorry," she whispered, patting the horse's neck. "I'll give you a sugar cube when we're on the other side."

Storm clouds rumbled overhead as the path sloped upwards. The ground underfoot became rockier and more unstable. Eventually, her steed was unable to keep its footing appropriately and she had to dismount. She hugged her and whispered sweet words to her as she took off the saddle.

"Just in case I don't make it back," she whispered. She struck the horse on her rump and watched as she galloped away.

The path up the mountain was winding and steep. The ground crumbled beneath her feet as she began the upward trek. She quickly decided to leave her pack behind. It was too heavy and left her off-balance too much. She took only what she needed: her weapons and her small satchel of herbs and potions. She prayed the Light would provide anything else she needed.

By the time she reached the first plateau on the path, her calves were cramped and aching. She massaged them as she sat and drank deeply from her water skin. Her muscles quivered when she stood once more. She desperately wanted to sit down again, but she couldn't. She wanted to finish this. Even if it meant pushing herself to the breaking point. Besides, focusing on moving forward helped her not to think too long about Emma.

She was in the middle of a steep incline when her feet slipped on the rubble. She slid down the side of the mountain, gaining speed as she went Frantically, she tried to catch ahold of something—anything—to stop herself from going over the edge. Rocks sliced her hands, coating her fingers in blood, making them even slicker.

She grappled with her belt, trying to draw her dagger. Her feet skated over the edge of the mountain, nothing but a straight drop to the bottom to stop her. She screamed as she finally drew her blade and slammed it into the ground. It dragged in the soil for several seconds before coming to a stop. Iris hung from her dagger. Her arms shook as she tried to draw herself up.

She barely budged.

Screaming, she attempted to swing her legs to the side. If she could just get enough leverage, she was certain she could climb back onto the mountainside. Dust fell in her eyes, causing them to sting and water as her dagger loosened more of the soil.

She stopped swinging, afraid the movement would break off the bit of ground holding her dagger in place. She did not want to die here. Not when she was so close to finding Liam.

She breathed in deeply. Her muscles strained. A rush of adrenaline coursed through her as she lifted herself high enough to let go of the dagger with her right arm. She gripped the ledge and pulled herself the rest of the way up. She shook as she scooted away from the edge and pressed her back against the cool stone of the mountain.

She rested for a moment, needing to feel like she was secure, at least for a moment, before standing and continuing her trek up the mountain.

Soon, she was on her way again. Her body ached, but she refused to give in.

By the time she reached the cave mouth Grandmother Rel had indicated on the map she'd shown her in the dreamworld, Iris could barely move and collapsed onto the ground in a heap.

The sun was setting. Shadows stretched and writhed over the ground. Iris crawled to a small, withered tree and curled up beneath it. It wouldn't do her any good to confront Grandmother Rel if she couldn't even stand straight.

"I'm here, Liam," she whispered as she drifted off to sleep.

An intense burning woke her. She turned over, swatting her hands over her body as she attempted to make the sensation stop. Giant red ants crawled over her skin, leaving welts in their wake.

Iris rolled away, trying to squash them. They didn't die easily. She noticed that she'd been laying atop one of their mounds and groaned. Standing, she brushed off the ants. They bit her hands, making them ache and swell within seconds of their poison entering her system.

Her fingers shook as she fumbled with her potions satchel. She knew she had something in there would help with the burning and itching. She just needed to find it.

Her flesh was so swollen, she couldn't bend her fingers. Frustration mounted within her as she attempted to undo the satchel's clasp. With a growl, she dropped the satchel and kicked it.

Yelling at no one in particular, she slammed her hand into the mountain side. More pain flared up through her arms. She shook her hand trying to dull the agony.

It didn't help. If anything, it made it worse.

She dropped to the ground and pulled the satchel into her lap. Wedging it between her knees, she used her teeth to pull the drawstring clasp out until it was loose enough that she could open the top. She dumped the contents onto the ground as carefully as she could, praying none of the bottles broke as they landed on the hard surface.

Angry tears streamed down her cheeks as she sifted through the various bottles and jars. Finally, she found the one she was looking for. It was relatively small and indistinct compared to the others. A silver liquid filled it and swirled as she swished the bottle. Biting the cork stoppering it, she pulled it open, then drank the entire contents.

166

The relief it caused was instantaneous. She almost laughed. It had been Grandmother Rel who'd taught her that particular potion. She'd made Iris make it over and over again until she'd memorized the ingredients and gotten the brewing perfect.

Thank the Creators she had.

The swelling in Iris's hands decreased rapidly. She flexed her fingers. They were still stiff and ached whenever she tried to bend them past a certain point, but at least she could move them again.

She sighed, waiting for the potion to finish counteracting the ants' poison.

A cool breeze grazed her cheeks as she stared off the mountain edge and out over the whole of Dramadoon. Mountain peaks crested white, fluffy clouds. Smoky hues of purple, pink, blue, and orange swept over the forest below her, giving the whole scene a surreal, dreamlike quality. A sense of calm settled on her as she watched the sun rise over the eastern peaks and bathe her kingdom in a soft, golden haze.

She understood why Emma had left her then.

She wanted to fight for this. To save something more than just a single life. Even if it meant abandoning her, Iris understood. More than anything, she wished she could tell her sister that.

Shaking her head, she swept the remaining bottles back into her satchel and slung it over her shoulder. She faced the cave mouth. It was a new day. Her head still ached, and she didn't know if she would ever be able to ease the tension in her muscles again, but if she didn't enter the belly of the beast now, she didn't think she ever would.

Setting her jaw, she took the first step into the cave.

She had expected the cave to be cool. Instead, it was more sweltering than it had been outside. Iris shed layers of her clothing as she descended deeper into the mountain.

She didn't know how far she needed to go. Grandmother Rel's directions only guided her to the cave mouth, not beyond.

Her feet ached as she kept going. She had no concept of how long she had been walking. She thought it could have been hours or days. Her calves continued to quake with each step, and she knew she would struggle to stand again if she took a moment of reprieve.

So, she kept going.

Torches illuminated the walkway. It was as if Grandmother Rel knew exactly when she was arriving and prepared for her. Iris didn't know if that brought her comfort or more anxiety.

She rounded a bend in the path and knocked into something hard and metal. She shrieked as she stumbled backwards and landed on her rump. A coat of armor was set up in the middle of the room. Scorch marks marred the metal.

She reached for her daggers, anticipating an attack that never came. Blinking up at the suit of armor, she kicked at it with her boot. It rattled hollowly. She breathed out a sigh of relief and leapt to her feet.

Tentatively, she lifted the helm's visor. A skull stared back at her. She screeched and stumbled backwards. Her heart raced as, for the first time since entering the cave, she looked down.

Her eyes widened as she took in the path. Bones lined the pathway. They were so perfectly aligned on the walkway that there was no way they had naturally fallen there. Someone had taken a lot of time—or a lot of magic—to create the trail framed in bone. Gulping, she leaned down to try and tell if they were human or animal.

It was a mixture, if she had to guess.

She rose quickly and skirted her way around the armor.

Her footsteps echoed loudly down the path. The walls sparkled in the torchlight. She trailed her fingers over them, realizing that they were covered in thousands of crystals. A rainbow of color stretched down the path. If she weren't walking to her potential doom, she might have found the scene beautiful. As it was, it only reminded her that she might never see a rainbow again.

A boney hand grasped her wrist and yanked her around. She attempted to slam one of her daggers into it, but the blade clinked against bone. She screamed when she saw the skull, still wearing the helm, smile at her.

The skeletal knight threw Iris into a dungeon. Its eyes flashed ruby as it turned the key in the padlock and stalked away.

Iron bars, too narrow for her to fit through, lined her cell. Regardless, she flung herself against them, hoping she could tear them down with her weight and momentum.

She bounced back, her chest and ribs screaming in pain at being smacked against the bars. The prison didn't even rattle.

She tried slipping her arm through the bars to finger the lock. She thought she had a pin in her satchel that would work nicely as a picklock. She'd never successfully picked a lock before, but she was game to try.

Her arm was too big to maneuver through the bars.

Crying out in frustration, she sank to the ground and tried to think. Angry tears streamed down her cheeks. Emma had been right.

It had been a trap.

"You're alone?" Grandmother Rel's voice echoed through the bars.

Iris jerked her head towards the sound, but saw nothing.

"Maybe," she said.

"You are," Grandmother Rel replied, humor in her tone. "Wherever has my least favorite granddaughter gone?"

"Maybe she's waiting outside the cave, waiting for me to return to her," Iris said. There was a chance, however, small, that she wasn't lying.

"She's not," Grandmother Rel said. "I would be able to sense her if she was."

Iris shrugged.

"You don't know everything, Grandmother," she whispered.

Grandmother Rel's eyes glowed in the darkness and smoke curled from her nostrils. Iris resisted the urge retreat. She forced herself to lift her chin and meet her gaze head on.

"I used to be so afraid of you," she said. "I used to think that your disappointment in me was the worst thing that could ever happen to me." With each word she spoke, she realized how far she'd come since her in isolation in Grandmother Rel's cabin. "But now I see. It was you who should have been afraid of me."

Grandmother Rel stepped into the light. Her creamy, smooth skin wrinkled as she frowned.

"Why would I ever be afraid of a slip of a girl like you?" she hissed.

Iris laughed. "You forget that you raised me. I know your weaknesses."

Grandmother Rel snarled. "You know only what I chose to reveal to you, girl." She spun around. "Look at me now. Younger, more beautiful than ever. My coven won't recognize me when I seize back control." She leaned into the bars as she spoke and smiled viciously at Iris. "I suppose I do owe you a bit of gratitude. You have successfully disbanded the strength of the coven who wanted to kill me."

Iris balled her hands into fists and stood so that her face was only separated from Grandmother Rel's by the bars.

"You're a coward," she said. "You let others do your dirty work for you because you're too afraid to dirty your hands."

"I'm smart," Grandmother Rel corrected. "And if you had a half a brain, you'd see that I did what I had to survive."

"By the stars, Grandmother! Do you even hear yourself right now? You didn't have to raise us in isolation. You didn't need to steal Emma's youth to replenish your own. You didn't need to take Liam from me. You made those choices. No one else. And, you will pay for them in the end."

Grandmother Rel placed her hand on her cheek and tapped a long nail. "It strikes me that you aren't grateful for everything that I've done for you. I tried to be a good caretaker. I tried to show you how much I care for you." She reached her fingers through the bars and grazed Iris's cheeks. "You were always my favorite, Iris. Always so... submissive. Eager to please me. It wasn't until you met Liam in your dreams that you began to pull away from me."

Her nails raked across Iris's flesh, leaving tiny pink lines on her otherwise porcelain skin. Iris jerked backwards, pressing her hand against the scratches.

Grandmother Rel sighed. "I've decided to show you just how much I am willing to do for you, dear one." Her lips curled in a dark, sly smile. "Liam was nothing more than a plaything for me, and I grow tired of his incessant thoughts of *you*." More smoke billowed from her nostrils. "But as I said, I am willing to forgive you. I am even willing to give him back to you."

Iris stared at Grandmother Rel, hope swelling inside in. She didn't like the tone she was using and was wary of bargain she attempted to make, but she was so desperate to see Liam, to know that he was okay, that she was willing to make any deal necessary to do so.

"Prove your loyalty to me and I promise you can have him back. I'll even give him to you unscathed." She smirked. "Of course, his memories of his broken body and hours of torture will be yours to deal with."

Iris flung herself towards the bars and forced her arms through them. She attempted to grab Grandmother Rel, to strangle her. To make her know just how much she hated her.

Grandmother Rel took a single step backwards and out of reach. Without another word, she turned to walk away.

"Let me see him!" Iris cried, giving in. "Please!"

"No."

The word hung in the air, suffocating, as Grandmother Rel disappeared into the shadows. Iris stood for several moments staring after her.

She wished, more than anything, that Emma was there with her.

Chapter Twenty

Emma

Wind whipped through Emma's hair as she rode hard down the forest path. She breathed in the hot, humid air and smiled. This was what true freedom felt like.

She closed her eyes for the briefest of moments, letting herself believe that she was soaring through the clouds, on her way to explore the world. She wanted to see it all. The ocean. The deserts. The islands. She wanted to travel beyond the unknown and discover for herself what mysteries resided there.

But first, she wanted to serve her kingdom. Chiara had been right. They needed to give all that they could for the good of the whole. Not just an individual.

Thoughts of Iris crept along the seams of her mind, attempting to drag her into self-doubt. She flicked them aside. There wasn't time for uncertainty. A darkness was growing. Iris had said so herself.

Things seemed to be clicking into place. The mysterious figures who'd attacked Iris and had been killing witches. The rumors they'd heard so long ago about the mad king. It all was part of a growing problem, even if she didn't entirely understand it yet.

She wanted to be a part of the solution.

And so, she rode.

Besides, Iris had told her to go. That she didn't need her anymore. Maybe she didn't. It had been Iris who had saved them so often over the past several months. She didn't have any reason to doubt that her sister would find a way to free Liam from Grandmother Rel and come to the capital.

You're stronger together, a nagging voice whispered at the back of her mind. Emma sighed. She knew that was the truth, too.

But there was nothing she could do about it.

When it came to Liam, Iris was irrational.

She pulled back on the reins, slowing her mount's pace, and turned in the saddle to see if Micah had been able to keep up with her. His long hair was tousled and framed his face in a halo of dark curls. He smiled at her and her heart skipped a beat.

"Are you riding towards or away from something?" he asked.

Emma pulled her horse to a halt and met his gaze. "What are you talking about?"

He brought his mount up beside her and took her reins from her. "You come storming into my tent, saying that you're leaving and that I can choose who to go with: you or Iris. You gave no explanation. Just an ultimatum." He tucked a lock of her hair behind her ear and smiled at her. "As if I ever had a choice."

She raised her eyebrows at him and blinked in an exaggerated fashion. "You did have a choice," she said with a curt smile. "And you chose wrong."

S.A. McClure

She yanked her reins out of his and pushed her horse into a canter. Conflicted emotions coursed through her. She wanted him to be with her, but she couldn't stop herself from feeling angry at him for letting Iris go off on her own. Of course, she knew her anger was more directed at herself than it was at him. But, she couldn't tell him that. Not yet, anyway.

The path was just wide enough for them ride together side-by-side.

"Do you even know why you left her?" he asked.

She whipped her head towards him, a snarl on her face. Her retort died on her lips when she saw a dark shadow in the trees behind him, keeping pace with them. She opened her mouth to scream as the spider leapt from the trees and landed atop Micah.

For a moment, Emma continued riding, too shocked to react. Then, Micah's screams broke through her thoughts and she turned her horse around. Reaching into her pocket, she drew the bow Eldridge had given her and pulled an arrow from her quiver.

Her mind cleared as she rode past the giant spider pinning Micah to the ground. Thick saliva dripped from its pinchers as it attempted to bite him. His arms trembled as he held it back. Thick strands of white silk curled around Micah's legs, nearly immobilizing him.

She inhaled as she aimed, letting her muscle memory take over, and she exhaled and released the arrow. She didn't wait to see if she hit her mark as she drew another one and fired again. And then a third time.

Black, goopy blood oozed from the puncture wounds, extinguishing the arrows' flames. They did nothing to stop the spider's attack on Micah. She rounded the other side of the spider, searching the tree line for any sign that there were others. She'd read once that they liked to live in colonies.

She prayed to the Creators that the books had been wrong.

She reached for another arrow to find that she only had two left. She shook her head and reprimanded herself for not taking the time to make another set of them. Arrows stuck out from the spider's body, making it look like a pincushion. Despite the blood seeping from its wounds, it didn't seem to be taking any notice of the arrows at all.

Her hand trailed along the hilt of the elfish dagger. She could plunge the onyx blade deep into its belly. Rid it of its essence. The dagger seemed to call to her as she held it grasped within her fist. She drew it, her hand shaking, and she peered at her reflection in its dark blade.

"Emma! Run!" Micah screamed, drawing her attention.

She glanced up in time to see that another spider was leaping from high above her. Saliva dripped onto her forehead. She didn't have time to contemplate whether using the blade was the Light's will or an action of Darkness. Clutching the hilt with both hands, she jutted the dagger into the air, letting the spider impale itself upon the onyx blade.

Its weight was almost overwhelming. She fell from her horse as the spider landed atop her. It twitched for several moments and she twisted her hands. It stilled, its full weight crushing her, before flopping onto its back, its legs curling inward.

Panting, she forced herself to ignore her disgust of the beast as she climbed atop it to wrench the dagger free.

She didn't have time to think about what she'd just done. Micah had gone silent and his safety became her top priority. She wiped the spider's ichor covering the blade on the leaves covering the ground before racing towards the spider pinning Micah.

She leapt onto its back with a scream. Its pinchers clicked and its entire body shook as it tried to shake her off. She wrapped her legs around its body as much as she could and squeezed. Its head rotated around until its multiple eyes met hers. She saw her anger, her vengeance reflected in its face as she slammed the dagger into its back.

She ripped the dagger free and leapt from the spider's back. She rolled as she landed on the ground, then sprang to her feet and rushed to Micah. He was completely encased in the spider silk.

She dropped the onyx dagger to the ground and fumbled with the blade sheathed at her hip. Her hands shook as she sliced the silk down the middle. She moved slowly so as not to cut him in the process.

His skin was strangely pale as she cut away the last remnants of the silk. His lips were tinged blue.

"No," she whispered, laying her head down on his chest.

At first, she didn't hear anything above the pounding of her own heart. She closed her eyes and focused on calming herself. She breathed in deeply. And then she felt it. The slow, shallow rise and fall of his chest as he breathed.

She wrapped her arms tight around his chest. Her entire body shook as she cried tears of relief. She kissed his forehead. His cheeks.

His lips.

He didn't stir as she sat back on her haunches.

She'd never kissed anyone before other than her sister. She trailed her fingers of her lips and cringed. He was basically a corpse. Great. How was she going to explain this to him?

She started to crawl back to him. Rustling in the trees issued from just beyond the dead spider's body. Reaching out, she grasped the onyx blade's hilt and crouched beside Micah.

She scanned the trees lining the path. Shadows writhed as the wind shook the leaves and birds hopped from branch to branch. It seemed strange to her that birds would still be alive with predatory spiders in the area.

It struck her that she didn't hear birdsong. Or the chatter of squirrels or chipmunks. In fact, as she listened closely, she didn't hear the sounds of any forest animals.

She tilted her head back and stared skyward. Her heart stopped as she saw more spiders dropping from the sky. The onyx blade wouldn't be enough to fend them off alone. There were three of them. One was larger than the two who had already attacked them. The other two were significantly smaller. Her skin crawled as she watched them descend.

She hated spiders.

They really were the only thing in the forest that she absolutely loathed above anything else.

She glanced around the path. Both horses were gone. She assumed they'd fled during the first round of attacks. Although she wished they were still there so that they might've had a chance to outrun the spiders, she hoped that, wherever they were, they were safe.

She flipped the dagger in her hand and crouched on the balls of her feet, ready to spring forward. It was already an unfair fight, made worse by the fact that she had no doubt they would attack her all at once.

Sweat slid down her brow and into her eyes, stinging them. She blinked rapidly, trying to ease the pain.

The first spider fell the remaining feet to the ground and landed with a reverberating thud. It clicked its pinchers, its multiple eyes angry and intelligent. Emma backed away to find that the second of the spiders had swung above her and was now behind her. The third blocked the path to her right.

She silently prayed to the Light that she and Micah would survive to see another day before sprinting forward. She pushed down with her feet just as she leapt forward and landed on the spider's head. Swallowing her urge to scream, she jabbed the dagger into one of the spider's eyes. Its pinchers closed around her thigh.

She screamed. The spider's saliva mixed with her blood, numbing her. A sinking realization struck her then. She remembered that the spiders were supposed to be able to paralyze their victims by introducing their saliva to their prey's bloodstream.

She jabbed her finger into another of the spider's eyes and it released her. She pulled the dagger free and jammed it into the spider's forehead. It fell backwards, curling up as it went.

She leapt from its body and landed on her injured leg. She cried out in pain and tumbled to the ground.

The two smaller spiders advanced towards her. They seemed scared to approach her, yet there was a fire in their eyes that told her they were void-bent on extracting their revenge for what she'd done to their family. They shared a look with each other before staring her down and then deliberately turning their attention to Micah. They crawled toward him.

"Stay away from him!" she shouted. She attempted to stand but neither of her legs wanted to work. The spider's venom was already coursing through her body. Slowing her heartbeat.

If she passed out now, while the two remaining spiders were still alive, she would be dead. Micah would be dead, too.

She couldn't let that happen. Digging her nails into the soil, she dragged herself forward. Blood seeped from the ridges of her nails as they broke. She ignored the pain in her hands and the numbness creeping up her body.

She refused to let them turn her into prey.

She was a huntress. She always had been.

They were biting him. Deep bruises formed on his skin as they sucked blood from him. They were so consumed by their meal they didn't notice when she reached one of them. She jammed the dagger into its leg. It hissed in pain as she wrenched the blade free and plunged in into its backside. Like the others before it, it writhed for several moments before falling onto its back, its legs curling into its chest.

Emma couldn't feel her abdomen. Or her chest.

She knew her arms would come next.

The remaining spider whipped its head towards her. Its pinchers dripped a mixture of Micah's blood and its saliva as it lunged for her. Emma didn't think. She just reacted. She threw the dagger at the spider, praying to the Light that it sank into its heart. That she would be safe.

The venom coursed through her veins and she fainted.

Chapter Twenty-One

The skeletal knight guided Iris into a room she immediately recognized as Grandmother Rel's potions room. Jars of various ingredients lined one wall and a long, wooden table rested in the middle of the space. A myriad of mixing bottles, mortars, pestles, and measuring spoons lay on the table in disarray. A wall of shelves contained fully brewed potions. Iris scanned their labels, searching for poisons, but found none.

She didn't know if she was relieved or disappointed. On the one hand, that most likely meant that Grandmother Rel didn't intend to poison her. On the other, she couldn't try to sneak a bottle out of the room to use against the hag later.

"My dear, sweet child," Grandmother Rel said as she entered the room.

Iris jumped. She hadn't heard her coming.

"Grandmother Rel," she said, bobbing her head at the woman.

The witch's lips curled into a hard, thin smile. "You don't seem pleased to be here," she said, pouting. "This whole time, ever since I left you in that ravine, all I've been able to think about is being a family again."

"What family?" Iris muttered.

Grandmother slapped her, hard, across the cheek. Her eyes flashed crimson as she brought her hand up to do it again.

"*Our* family," she hissed. "You, me, and Emma. I miss you both dearly."

Although her cheek stung, Iris met Grandmother Rel's gaze with any icy one of her one. "We were never a family, Myrella."

Using her given name instead of 'grandmother' felt strange on Iris's tongue, but she didn't want to use that term anymore. She was not and never had been her grandmother.

Myrella's cheeks turned a putrid shade of red as she stared Iris down. "Your sister has had such a bad influence on you," she said. "I will have to punish her when she comes for you."

Iris blinked. "What do you mean, when she comes for me? Emma isn't coming here. She left to join the fight with the royal family."

"They are fools," Myrella sighed. "They always have been."

"I thought you were their friend. A trusted advisor?" she asked.

Myrella shrugged. "Loyalty to the crown is like a breeze during summer. Fleeting."

Iris didn't know how to respond, so she didn't say anything at all.

Myrella clapped her hands and smiled at Iris. "I thought it would be nice if we could brew a potion together. Just like the old days."

There was something about the way she said it that made Iris
distrust her intentions.

"What do you really want?" she asked, raising an eyebrow.

"I told you, prove your loyalty to me—"

"How?" Iris asked. "How am I supposed to 'prove' my loyalty
to you?"

"There is a little task I need you to complete."

"Of course there is," Iris said. "What is it?"

Myrella didn't respond immediately. Instead, she hummed to
herself as she crossed the room and pulled ingredients from their
shelves. She laid them on the table. Iris read each handwritten
label, her stomach sinking as she realized the ingredients could
only be for one of a handful of potions.

"What do you intend to make?" she asked tentatively. Her
cheek still burned from where she'd been slapped, and she was
reticent to anger Myrella further.

"It's a summoning potion."

"A dark one," Iris responded.

Myrella paused, her fingers wrapped around a rat's skull. She
cocked an eyebrow at Iris and asked, "When has that ever stopped
you before?"

Iris scrunched up her face in confusion. "What are you talking
about?"

"We've been brewing dark potions since you were the wee
age of nine," Myrella said with a smile. "You never noticed how
we changed books periodically? How some pages were ornately
decorated with whimsical, happy things while others were
dedicated to the darker side of life?"

Iris shook her head.

"Yes, well, you never were one to recognize things outside of
your tunnel vision."

Iris didn't like the fact that she'd unwittingly created potions
that were steeped in Darkness. She exhaled through her nose to
keep herself from saying something she would regret.

"Can I see Liam?" she asked instead. She didn't know if
pressuring Myrella to let her see him would anger the witch or

not, but she didn't care. She hadn't been able to stop thinking about him the entire night she'd been locked in the cell. He deserved to know that she'd come for him.

"The answer is still no, Iris. If you ask again, I will retract my offer and you will never see him again."

Iris sputtered. She'd come so far to be here. She'd lost Emma. For him. So that she could rescue him.

Iris met Myrella's gaze and smiled. "I understand. You will let me see him in your own time."

"I promise."

She trusted Myrella's promises as far as she could throw them, which was nowhere.

"What do you want me to do?" she asked again.

"Oh, that," Myrella replied nonchalantly. "I want you to find someone in the dreamworld for me. Goes by the name of Rhys. You may find him as Maldy."

"Wouldn't a job like this be better suited for Emma?" she asked before she could stop herself. She clamped her hand over her lips before she could utter another word. She'd forgotten that Myrella had already abandoned them by the time Emma realized she had powers.

Myrella leaned forward, her eyes narrowed as she whispered, "Why?"

Iris thought about lying for about two seconds before realizing that this was probably part of the test.

"Emma can track people using magic."

"She's a Starseeker? Really?" Myrella asked, rubbing her chin. "Tell me more."

Iris didn't want to. In fact, there was nothing she wanted less at that precious moment than to tell the hag about the full extent of her or Emma's abilities.

She shrugged. "There's not much to tell, really. Sometimes, she can just sense where people are."

Myrella frowned. "That's all?" she asked. "No other senses?"

"Not that I'm aware of."

"She always was the weaker of the two of you."

Iris started to defend Emma. Her sister had always been strong and protective. She had provided for them, even in the darkest and coldest of winters. What had Iris done? Brewed potions and acquiesced to each of Grandmother Rel's commands.

She hands tightened into fists the more she thought about everything Emma had done for them.

"But, as I was saying, you are the dreamwalker, Iris. No one else can find him for him other than you." She pointed to a jar on the table.

"And once I find him, what am I supposed to do?" she asked. Her hands shook as she picked up the jar and dumped the contents into a mortar. Little ivory bones clinked in the stone bowl. She looked away as she ground them into a fine powder using the pestle.

"Give him a message for me," Myrella said. "Tell him that he is welcome to join me here, in Dramadoon. Tell him that I can offer protection to him. Shelter from the growing storm."

"Who is he to you?" Iris asked. The last time she'd agreed to find someone in the dreamworld, she'd nearly died for her troubles. Of course, that all might have been part of Elilda's plan.

"He is…" Myrella paused as she sniffed at a bottle of a strange, silvery liquid. "He is an old friend."

"You don't have any friends beyond your coven members." Iris said as she dropped in a handful of bitter smelling leaves. They released a rotten smell as they mixed with the other ingredients. Myrella placed a pair of bat wings on the table along with a few jars containing herbs and parts of dead animals. "And, since you said Rhys is a 'he,' I'm going to assume he's not one your members. So, tell me who he is, really."

"You're too smart for your own good, dearie."

"So, who is he?" Iris repeated. She stirred the potion according to Myrella's instructions.

"You've certainly grown more persistent since we last saw one another," she hissed.

Iris cringed, anticipating the blow that didn't come. She stole a glance at Myrella to find her staring at her with a curious expression on her face.

"As I said, he's an old friend. He's in a spot of trouble and I would like to him through it, if I can. We all must follow the Light's path."

"You swear he won't hurt me when I find him?" she asked.

"I can't swear to it, no, but I can promise you this. If he does, I will revoke my offer of aid."

"That's just so comforting," Iris retorted. "If I end up dead, you'll be sure to extract your revenge by simply not helping him. Got it. And here I thought you were a cold, savage killer."

Myrella cackled. "I see you've gained a sense of humor," she said. Her expression turned serious as she added, "If you die, I promise I'll take care of Emma."

Iris rolled her eyes. "She doesn't want you anywhere near her, so no, you won't be taking care of her. If I die, I want you to promise me you'll leave her alone." She paused, her thoughts zipping through her mind in rapid succession. "And I want you to release Liam without further harming him."

"Done."

She'd agreed too easily, Iris realized. She should have asked for more.

"So, how do we do this?" she asked.

The potion they were making began to bubble. It went from a vibrant violet color to a thick black goo.

"Drink this before you enter the dreamworld," Grandmother Rel commanded. "And I promise you, it'll help you find him."

Iris cocked an eyebrow at the potion. It smelled like a rotting animal that had been left out in the open for too long. She could imagine the swarm of flies, the gangrene flesh, and the maggots.

"No," she said. She crinkled her nose in disgust and frowned. "There's absolutely no way I'm going to drink that."

"Yes, you are. That is, if you ever want to see your precious Liam ever again."

Iris glared at Myrella. She knew how to manipulate her into doing whatever it was she wanted. She always had, even when Iris had been a little girl.

Iris took a deep breath. "Fine."

"Excellent," Myrella said, clapping her hands. "I'm so glad you've decided to do the right thing." She dipped a portion of foul-smelling potion into a cup and handed it to Iris. "Bottoms up, dearie."

Iris pinched her nose so that she wouldn't have to smell the potion as she drained the contents in a single gulp. It burned going down and she felt as if her chest were on fire when it finally hit her stomach. She belched loudly.

"What's it supposed to do?" she asked, realizing she hadn't done that before.

"When you enter the dreamworld, the potion will aid you in finding Rhys. I can't promise what he'll be in. I hear he's been quite… aggressive since coming back."

Iris didn't care where he'd been or why he was back. She did, however, care about the fact that Myrella had described him as aggressive. Too late now, she supposed.

"Good to know," she said. She closed her eyes and eased herself into the dreamworld.

Chapter Twenty-Two

Iris

Iris landed in an unfamiliar place for the second time in only a few days. Skeletons laid crumpled on the ground, their helms and suits of armor battered. Dust swelled into roaring funnels as wind swept across the relatively flat terrain. She shielded her face with one hand to try and block the particles from scratching her eyes.

She peered behind her to find a narrow, stone bridge stretching across marshland. Smoke and shadows shrouded the walkway. It disappeared into the distance with no endpoint in sight.

She wasn't sure if she was supposed to cross the bridge or wander deeper into the graveyard before her to find Rhys.

Sighing, she took a step towards the bridge. It didn't have a railing on it and Iris knew that if she stumbled even the slightest bit while crossing, she would plunge to her death. She glanced over her shoulder, hoping that the potion would guide her back to the battlefield.

It didn't.

She placed one foot on the bridge and instantly felt a sharp tug at her navel. The world swirled around her in a blur of color. It was like a tornado of sensations pulsing within her. She pressed her hands to her eyes to block out the light as dizziness enveloped her.

She landed in shallow water. Sea foam fizzed at her feet and a cool breeze kissed her skin. A lone cottage rested on a peak further down the beach. A curl of smoke plumed from its chimney. Although her head still ached and she felt jittery, Iris trekked towards the cottage.

"Hello?" she called as she stepped on the porch. Long, strong beams had been constructed underneath to provide support to the structure. It hung out over the cliff so that, when she looked over the railing, all she could see was the swell of the ocean.

"What are you doing here, girl?" a ruff voice asked from within the cottage. She whirled around, her back pressing firmly into the railing.

A tall man with bronze skin and dark hair stood before her. Veins bulged in his muscles even when he wasn't moving. She had no doubt that he could crush her with a single flex. She gulped.

"I'm looking for someone who goes by the name of Rhys?" she muttered. "Or Maldy? Oh, I don't know!"

He crossed powerful arms over his chest and smiled at her.

"And what would a sweet, little thing like you be doing looking for a beast like him?" he asked. There was laughter in his words that made Iris take a second look at him.

Although he was tall, muscular, and intimating, his face was also kind. His eyes held a sadness in them that gave Iris pause.

"I was sent to offer aid," she said.

He smiled at her. "You best be coming in then."

He turned his back on her, clearly fully confident that she would be joining him in the cottage. She glanced out at the sea, breathing in the salty air. The world here seemed fresh. Untouched by war. Ignorant of the ways of men. It was nice.

She followed him into the cottage.

"Who sent you?" he asked as he lit several candles all around the room with a snap of his fingers.

"Myrella Dimati."

His eyes grew wide. "I haven't heard that name in a while," he muttered. "How is the old broad?"

"You do know her, then?" she asked, cocking an eyebrow. "I didn't think she had any friends outside of the coven."

He shook his head. "I wouldn't consider us friends, exactly. I have watched her since she was a small child. She showed great potential."

"Oh, so you're older than you look, then."

He chuckled at her. "Yes, I am quite the old fart, if you ask me." He stretched and, to her astonishment, his muscles bulged even more. He gave her a lazy smile. "Tell me more about her offer."

"Well, for starters, she said that you could join her in Dramadoon. That she could provide you shelter from the storm."

His shoulders hunched as she spoke, his facial features contorting into what can only be described as rage. He stumbled towards a wardrobe and flung open the doors. Iron shackles hung from a peg on the inside door. He locked them around his wrists and throat with a loud snap before turning to face her.

"Run," he whispered. "Hide. This shouldn't last more than a few moments."

"What shouldn't last more than—" She clamped her lips shut as his nose elongated into a snout. His hazel eyes turned golden and his canines lengthened into sharp points.

She stepped backwards, too shocked to react. He howled at her, his eyes darkening with desire.

She turned and ran.

Rhys lunged for her, a vicious cry on his lips. Iris cowered behind a table. She squeezed her eyes shut, not wanting to see how close he was to her body. How close she was to his death.

He released a strangled cry as the manacle around his throat cut off his airflow. He reached his arms out to her, attempting to snag her with one of his claws.

She leapt out of the way just as his nails raked across the spot she had just been sitting. He reached for again, but this time, he was too far away to reach her. Iris sighed in relief as she pressed herself against one of the windows and prayed the bonds would hold him.

His shoulders quaked and his snout began to shrink and morph back into human features. He slumped to the ground, trembling.

Although she was still afraid of him, Iris rushed forward and cradled his head in her hands.

"Are you alright?" she whispered. "You had me worried there for a moment."

He smiled up at her and placed a warm, firm hand on her cheek. "I would never want to cause a lass as beautiful as you a stitch of harm," he whispered. "You are like sunshine on a winter day."

"Thank you for that, I guess," she said as she checked him for wounds. The skin around his neck was rough and swollen, but she didn't see any reason to be concerned. It was obvious this had happened to him before.

"You should wrap in the chains in cloth if you want to avoid injuries like this in the future," she said, grazing her fingers over the swollen flesh at his wrists.

"You didn't come here to be a nursemaid to a tired, weak, old man," he said. "Who is Myrella Dimati to you?" he asked, his voice taking on a bitter edge.

She wasn't sure how to respond to that. Six months ago, she would have said that she had been like a mother to her, despite the name they called her. She would have described loving the woman for everything she'd done for them. Although she took them in out of selfish desire, she had still chosen to raise them. To provide for them. To teach them things that allowed them to survive.

She had given them a gift. This drive to keep pushing. To keep surviving.

To do it together.

The thought sent a pang of regret through Iris. They had done it all together. Until now.

Until she'd chosen to abandon her sister in order save Liam.

The muscles in her neck twitched as she met Rhys's gaze. "She raised me from a small child."

"That doesn't sound like the Myrella I know."

"How long ago did you interact with her?" she asked.

He paused, his features slackening. "Honestly, time is such a subjective concept that I can't pinpoint when I last met with her."

"How is that even possible?" Iris asked.

"Time is a construct we use to organize events in our lives. Mine has stretched for millennia All that is happening now has surely happened before and will happen again." He smiled at her with such sadness in his eyes that her heart felt like it was filling with water. The pressure in her chest was so tight she didn't know what to say to him. "If I know Myrella, then I know she's done something to force you to come here. What is it?"

Iris blinked at him. "How did you know?"

"As I said, all that has happened before is happening again. My sisters and brothers will not rest until they find me." He came to stand by her.

They stared out the large window facing the ocean. Waves lapped against the shore in rhythm with the world. It was calming.

"I came here to escape them. They nearly killed me once." His voice grew solemn. "They used someone too naïve to recognize just how much of his choice they'd already claimed for themselves. I couldn't get through to him." He sighed. "There are times when I hope I can face him again. Tell him that I forgive his role in trapping me. Perhaps the Darkness would not have consumed the world if I had done a better job at convincing him to follow a different path."

Iris watched him from the corner of her eye. What he was saying was nonsense. He spoke in obscurities.

"Who are you, really?" she asked.

"Rhys."

"I don't think so," she said. She turned to face him from the front. "There's something neither you nor Myrella have told me. Why don't you tell me now?"

He shook his head. "Let's strike a bargain, you and I. Tell me what she has on you and I promise I'll give you a clue as to who I am."

"A clue?" she said, crossing her arms over her chest. "Should I just give you a clue as to what she has on me then?"

He laughed. "No. I want the full story on that one."

She thought about it for a moment. If she was going to get Liam back, she needed to be able to tell Myrella that Rhys had, at the very least, considered her offer.

"Fine," she said, sticking her hand out for him to shake. He took it without a moment's hesitation. "A little over six months ago, I discovered I had the ability to dreamwalk." Her voice shook as she spoke, and she paused to get a grip on her emotions. "I met someone while I was there. A boy, Liam." She whispered his name.

"You love him," Rhys said. "Of course." He nodded as if this was nothing new and motioned for her to continue.

"He was cursed. His orders were to help monsters kill my sister and me. He chose to help us instead. I discovered a way to break the curse and set him free, so I did. Only then, he left with Myrella. He chose her over me."

"I see," Rhys said, meeting her gaze. His eyes undulated between gold, brown, and hazel as he stared at her. He smirked. "She probably gave him a love potion to make him leave with her. Classic Myrella." He frowned. "I never should have told her about that trick."

"That's terrible!" Iris cried. "How could you ever—"

"It's quite effective in being able to manipulate others into doing your bidding." He laughed softly to himself. "Let me guess, he appeared to you in the dreamworld and made you think he'd been tortured by her?"

"How—"

He slapped his hands on the window, a wide smile blossoming over his face. "I knew it!" He let out a gleeful laugh. "I'm not sure why. I don't have nearly the power I used to without my hammer, but I suppose, especially if we can find my sister, that we will be able to do something to help Light triumph after all."

Iris tuned him out as he continued to ramble. She didn't understand half the things he was saying and, if she was being honest, she didn't care. She just wanted him to agree to come to Myrella's mountain cave in the real world. That was it.

"Look," she said, "I don't know what you've been through in the past, but it sounds like a lot. All I know is that Myrella is offering you shelter. And, if you are willing to, at the very minimum, consider her offer, then she'll release Liam to me. So, what are you going to do?"

He stared at her for several moments without talking and then sighed heavily. "Tell Myrella that I will find her in the days to come."

He placed both his hands on her shoulders and kissed her brow. Warmth spread from her head to her toes and she felt her body dissolving as she was forced out of the dream.

"I hope we meet again," he whispered as he pulled back. "Until then, trust no one but yourself."

Iris coughed as she woke from the dream. She could still feel his lips on her brow. His last warning to her whirred in her mind as she opened her eyes and met Myrella's gaze.

Chapter Twenty-Three

Emma

Emma shuddered as she gained consciousness. Sweat coated her entire body, and her cotton underclothes clung to her beneath her leather armor. She groaned as she rolled over. She couldn't breathe, her chest was so tight.

"Micah?" she wheezed, sitting up. He lay an arm's length away, unconscious. She reached for his hand. "Micah!"

Blood covered soaked his clothes. There was a blue tinge to his skin and, when she grasped his hand, it was cold.

She flung herself atop his body.

"Please be alive," she whispered. "Please." She didn't want to beg, but she would if it meant that she could save him. She held her finger under his nose and waited.

She swore she felt the slightest movement of air on her finger, but she was terrified it was all her imagination. She couldn't hear his heartbeat. Or feel his chest rising and falling as he took in breath.

"You are not allowed to die on me!" she screamed as she slammed her fist into his chest. "Do you hear me? Do you!"

She hit him again.

His body jolted. She thought she heard a rib snap, but didn't give herself time to consider it. She just kept pumping his chest. It worked before. She'd been able to save Iris. She could save Micah.

She would.

More bones cracked under the force of her strikes. Still, he did not start breathing. She clutched his hand to her cheek. It was cold and limp.

"Micah," she whispered.

He did not respond.

She curled up next to him, not caring that his blood stained her clothes. Their horses were gone, and with them, their packs. They had nothing. She had nothing.

She didn't know how long she stayed beside him. How long she waited for any sign that he was breathing again. But, when she finally stood up, her back ached and her joints were still. The sister moons swelled within the sky, casting soft white light around the entire forest.

She kissed Micah's brow. His skin was still so cold. She lingered there, praying that she could bring life back to him. That she could heal him. She knew it was her imagination, but she could have sworn his skin warmed beneath her touch, as if she were transferring her heat to him.

With the moons shining down, the dead spiders looked even more creepy than Emma remembered. She kept her distance from their bodies. Although they weren't moving and she knew the onyx blade and ripped away their souls, they still made her skin crawl. Besides, Micah was dead because of them.

She stilled as the words reverberated through her.

Micah was dead.

She stared down at his body. She couldn't just leave him there. He deserved more than to be left for the scavengers to eat him. She searched the surrounding area until she found two tree limbs of relatively the same length. Using the silk she'd cut from his body, she stretched it between the two poles to create a stretcher. After laying his body on the silk, she began to pull him behind her.

As she walked, tears streamed down her cheeks. In her heart, she knew the stories were true. He'd saved her life countless times. He'd been there for her in moments when she most needed it. Even after Iris had broken his curse and he'd become human again, he'd stayed with her. Loyal to the end.

The moons sank and, in the east, a sliver of golden sun began to peek through the tree line. Her muscles hadn't fully recovered from the spiders' venom and her legs felt a little like jelly. She forced herself to place one foot in front of the other, though.

Her thoughts wandered to Iris. She hoped her sister had been able to make it to Grandmother Rel. She hoped she had been successful in freeing Liam. Her heart ached at the thought that they might not ever see one another again.

She glanced behind her. Micah was gone. That could have been her. She could've been the one on the stretcher.

She didn't know when she started, but she began running. Splinters dug into her palms as the twin poles jostled in her hands. She ignored the stabs of pain and continued going. Micah was heavy and her arms quivered, but she didn't stop.

Without a horse, she would never be able to catch up with Chiara and the elves. She longed to journey with them to the capital. To offer her services to the royal family. To make a meaningful contribution to the world. But now that Micah was dead—

The thought sent tremors coursing through her body. She wanted to cry. She wanted to beat herself for not protecting him.

For failing him.

"I'm so sorry," she whispered to his corpse.

Rain began to drizzle through the trees, soaking her clothes and making her shiver. She wanted to rest, but doing so could be a death sentence. Although she still had the bow, dagger, and dust from the elves, she didn't have any food, shelter, or way to make fire.

She trudged through the mud, wishing that she had gone with Iris. Then, at the very least, Micah would still be alive. It was her fault. If she hadn't convinced him to ride with her—

She dropped the stretcher's handles and knelt beside him. Even with the light rain, sunlight shined brightly through the trees. She wiped away a lock of his curly, dark hair and trailed her fingers over his face.

His skin seemed less blue and warmer than it had before. The humidity in the forest increased as the rain petered into mist.

Blisters covered her hands. She loathed picking up the handles again, knowing that multiple blisters would pop if she did so. She didn't want to see how deep the puss went. She'd once seen a man with a blister on his ankle so large that when he cut it open to release the pus, she could see the bone.

She cringed as the memory of the smell hit her. She refused to ever let her body deteriorate into such a state.

She stared at Micah for several moments, wishing she'd spent more time getting to know him post-humanization. He'd been kind to her, and she had treated him like filth. She leaned down and pressed her forehead against his.

"I wish things had been different, Micah. Mr. Wolf. Whatever your name was. I am sorry I kept you away."

A puff of air hit her lips. She jerked back in surprise. Her hands went out behind her to block her fall and her butt sank into the mud.

"What the—" she shouted.

Micah coughed.

Black mucus dripped from his lips and ran down his chin in a steady stream. Emma unsheathed the onyx dagger, ready to attack if he turned into an undead creature. Then his eyes fluttered open and he met her gaze, and she lowered her weapon.

"Micah!" She lurched towards him. She wrapped her arms tight around his middle and clung to him as he wheezed.

"Take it easy," he whispered. His voice was hoarse and strained.

When Emma pulled back, she was coated in his blood, which was now freely flowing from the puncture wounds at his neck and torso.

She didn't miss a beat. She took her leather jerkin off and slid out of her cotton undershirt. She ignored the fact that she was bare-chested in front of Micah. He needed something to stop the bleeding and this was the only option she had. The medical kit she'd assembled before the elves left had been on her horse.

She made quick work of tying the cloth around his wounds. He flinched when she pulled the ends taunt.

"Easy there," he said, placing a hand on the bandage. "I think you cracked my ribs when you tried to revive me."

"You knew I tried to start your heart again?" she asked.

She wondered what else he remembered. The memory of kissing him made her cheeks flush and she turned to peer into the trees. She pretended to scout for danger, but continued watching him from the corner of her eye.

"How?" she asked. "How is this possible?"

He chuckled softly, but then flinched as pain coursed through his body. He held his hands over his chest and side. "Spider venom slows the heart, remember?"

"Yes, but it only lasts for a short duration of time. I woke up hours ago."

"You also weren't almost completely devoured by a set of adolescent spiders void-bent on eating you alive," he retorted. "They bit me so many times, I'm half-surprised my heart started beating again, even if they didn't completely drain me."

She gripped his hands in her own.

"I'm glad it did," she whispered.

His eyes trailed over her face, lingering on her lips before they slipped downward. Emma blushed when she saw the hunger build in his eyes. She wrapped her arms over her chest and turned to her back to him, then slipped on her leather jerkin. It was rough against her skin, but she didn't care.

"Thank you," he whispered.

She cranked her neck around to look at him over her shoulder.

"For what?" she asked.

"For not leaving me behind. For thinking of me. For caring." He smiled at her.

She turned to face him fully and shrugged. "I couldn't leave you there, surrounded by dead spiders. If you'd died, it would've been my fault. I should never have—"

"I'm the one who chose to come with you, Emma. Besides, you couldn't have known that we'd be attacked by the spiders." He rubbed his chin and cocked an eyebrow at her. "Unless you did. In which case, it most definitely would've been your fault I almost died."

She flashed a half-smile at him. "You never know. I could be dangerous," she teased.

He laughed, then groaned and wrapped his hands around his middle again.

"We need to get you to a healer," she said, rising to her feet. She flexed her hands, preparing herself to pick up the poles again to drag Micah to the nearest village.

He caught her hand and turned it palm up. He frowned. Making a tsking sound, he turned his head upwards to look at her.

"I can walk," he said, voice low.

She shook her head. "No."

"Emma." He said her name like it was a delicate flower in full bloom. "I am a grown man who has been alive for over three hundred years. I think I can tell when I'm too weak to walk on my own two feet."

She looked everywhere but his eyes. She didn't want to risk his safety just so that the blisters on her hands wouldn't worsen.

He grimaced as he stood and then placed his hands on either side of her cheeks. "I know you feel guilty for not stopping the spiders before they injected me with their venom, but you don't have to worry about me. I can take care of myself."

"And what if I want to take care of you?" The words flowed out of her before she could stop them, and she turned away from him. Her cheeks burned.

He placed his hands on her shoulders and squeezed.

"We can take care of each other," he whispered. He leaned down and kissed the top of her head.

She didn't fight the tears as they streamed down her cheeks. She was just so relieved that he was alive. That she hadn't lost him before it was too late. She reached up and placed her hand atop his.

"We need to get moving," she said. "The sun will set soon, and we have a lot of ground to cover with how slowly you'll be moving."

She took a step away from him, creating space between them. Unsheathing one of her daggers, she bent down and cut the spiders' silk free from the poles. She folded it into a square and dropped it into her pocket, then headed down the path again.

"Emma," he said.

She turned to face him. "Micah?"

He met her gaze and held it. "I know you regret not going with Iris. You have to promise me that once we make it to a village, you'll find her. She needs you." He paused. "And you need her."

Emma stared at him for a moment. She didn't want to admit it, but he was right. No matter what happened, she would find Iris. They started this quest together and she would not let her sister finish it alone.

Golden light erupted from her chest, condensing into a vibrant line. She smiled as she shared a glance with Micah. She didn't know what the different colors of her abilities meant, but she knew one thing for certain: she would find Iris.

"Go," Micah whispered, as he grasped her hand. "Don't worry about me. I can find the village on my own." He squeezed her hand. "Besides, I know you will find me again."

She hesitated. Pain was etched across his face. She didn't want to leave him until she was certain that he would be cared for.

He shook his head at her. "I know what you're thinking, Emmaleigh. But please, don't worry about me. The most important thing you can do now is find Iris. Save Liam. Come back to me."

He lifted her fingers to his mouth and pressed his lips to her knuckles.

Emma relished the warmth that spread up her arm from the place his lips caressed her skin. She had never imagined that his kiss would be like this: full of hope, and a desire to continue caring for another person.

"I have to know——" she murmured

He wrapped his arms around her. She melted under his embrace.

"You'll know if I'm alive, Emma. You'll feel it here." He pressed his hand against her breast. "Now go."

This time, Emma didn't hesitate. She brushed a kiss over his mouth before darting into the trees.

Hours later, the warmth of him continued to linger on her as she followed the golden light leading to Iris. She just hoped she could find her before anything bad happened to her.

Chapter Twenty-Four

Emma

Emma stood at the cave entrance, the steady stream of golden light leading into the darkness beyond. It smelled foul down there and she was loath to enter. But she knew Iris was down there. Alone.

She drew the bow Eldridge had given her and strummed her fingers across the string. It reverberated as it grew into a full-size bow. Although it only took a few seconds for the bow to grow to its proper size, she didn't want to lose those precious seconds during a fight. She knew it could be the difference between life and death.

Inhaling deeply, Emma took her first step into the cave.

It began to shudder.

She raced down the wide, deep stairs. They were roughly cut from the mountain side. Emma wondered how many hours of manual labor were used to construct the lair, or if they had been built using magic.

Grandmother Rel's voice echoed through the cavern. Emma slowed her pace. She pressed her back against one of the cavern walls to block a surprise attack from behind. She inched her way down the stairs.

Peeking around the corner, she saw Grandmother Rel standing over Iris's unconscious body. Her eyes peered off into in the distance as if she were seeing something that no one else could. Her cheeks were pale and the stench of rotten eggs lingered in the air.

Smoke curled from the witch's nostrils. She appeared younger than Emma had ever seen her. She used to say that she believed using one's magic to keep oneself looking young was a waste. She vilified her coven members for their vanity. But here she was, with perfectly smooth skin, dark, luscious hair, and red lips.

Emma drew back on her arrow and aimed for Grandmother Rel's heart. Although she longed to lease the arrow, she hesitated. She didn't want to reveal herself until she knew she'd be able to get Iris out of this place alive.

She scanned the room. A suit of armor leaned against one wall. It didn't look like anyone was in it, but it was difficult to tell. Liam was nowhere to be seen. She half-expected him to be aligned with Grandmother Rel's plans. He'd seduced Iris. Made her believe that he cared for her. And, after she'd nearly died to save him, he had betrayed her.

She bit her bottom lip.

"Of course, my lady," Grandmother Rel whispered, bowing her head to some invisible force.

Emma squinted into the room, trying to determine if there was a shimmer of magic in front of Grandmother Rel or not. She didn't see anything. She strained her ears, waiting to hear if there was an answer. There was none, but Grandmother Rel continued talking.

"No need to worry about the girl. Once Rhymaldis has accepted my offer, I will kill her and be done with it."

Emma's heart skipped a beat. Was Grandmother Rel talking about Iris? And who was Rhymaldis? She'd never heard that name before.

"Yes, I know her powers would have been valuable to you, but we can all agree that she is too strong-willed to be allowed to live," Grandmother Rel said. "For all we know, she'd thwart our plans before we even had a chance to enact them."

Emma could not imagine who she was speaking with.

There was a pause and then she said, "The other one will not be a problem. I have her right where I want her. She will be little more than a worm wriggling on a hook when I'm done with her."

Emma's jaw clenched. She would never allow herself to be like a worm. She was a huntress. Not prey. Not bait. Anger rolled through her in powerful waves. She wanted nothing more than to run into that room and put a flaming arrow through the witch's throat.

But she stopped herself.

Iris was in there.

She needed to be smart about her attack. Grandmother Rel strong. She knew how to use magic in a way she'd never seen others use it. She was creative and vicious.

But she could be beaten.

Swallowing hard, Emma rounded the corner and sauntered towards Grandmother Rel, her bow still aimed straight at her heart.

"It's good to see you Grandmother Rel," she said as she lowered the bow.

The witch blinked rapidly, her eyes going from unfocused to aware. She scowled at Emma.

"What are you doing here?" she hissed.

Emma shrugged as she wandered over to a table and picked an apple out of a bowl. She wiped it on her sleeve before biting into it, juice spraying across the floor.

"I missed you," Emma said as she wiped her arm across the back of her face. She smiled. "I wanted to know if there was any way we could be a family again."

Grandmother Rel's eyes flashed between gold, red, and black. She made a low, guttural sound as she took a step towards Emma. More smoke billowed from her nostrils.

"Why are you really here?" she asked. "I thought you were on your way to the capital."

Emma shrugged. She wondered how Grandmother Rel knew that. Had Iris told her? She certainly hoped so. The alternative—that Grandmother Rel had been watching them—made her supremely uncomfortable.

She took another bite of the apple. "As I said," she replied with a full mouth, "I missed you."

Grandmother Rel's skin turned gray with black and red veins swirling across her flesh. Her feet rose from the ground. She stretched her hands out wide, her nails lengthening, turning to claws.

"You came here to kill me," she hissed. "Don't lie to me, Emmaleigh Valka. I raised you. I know you. I—"

"You're a fool, Grandmother Rel," Emma said.

Foolhardy or not, she was tired to Grandmother Rel's rants and monologues. She was a hag and nothing more.

Emma ducked in time to miss being hit by the fireball Grandmother Rel launched at her. She rolled across the floor and behind a chair. Breathing in deeply, she jumped up from her hiding place, aimed, and loosed her arrow, all within a manner of seconds. She didn't wait to see if the arrow struck home or not.

She only had a few arrows left in her quiver. She grasped one of them and waited for Grandmother Rel to approach. She watched as the witch's shadow grew smaller on the floor, indicating that she was drawing nearer.

She waited.

Her muscles were taunt and tense, ready to spring into action as she crouched behind the chair. The moment she saw the first tendrils of Grandmother Rel's magic curl around the edge of the chair, she leapt to her feet and fired.

The arrow exploded in a ray of sparks as it struck Grandmother Rel squarely in the chest. Blood bubbled around the wound and her lips gaped for several seconds before she fell backwards

Emma rushed to Iris and slapped her, hard, against the cheek. "Wake up," she whispered as she did it again. "Come on!"

"What are you doing?" Grandmother Rel hissed.

Emma looked over her shoulder in time to see Grandmother Rel advancing towards her. Her face was contorted with rage and her eyes gleamed gold as she sent a blast of energy at Emma.

She wasn't fast enough to block it. She was flung backwards. Her head slammed into the wall behind her. She yelped in pain and gingerly touched the spot that ached the worst. Her fingers came back coated in crimson blood.

"You think you can come here and ruin everything?" Grandmother Rel hissed. "I thought I'd got ridden of you." She growled. "The cockatrice was supposed to kill you!"

Emma whipped her head up. "You wanted me dead?"

She understood the words. But, even after everything the witch had done to her, she couldn't make herself believe that the woman who'd raised her wanted to end her.

Grandmother Rel rolled her eyes. "You really are the most pathetic—"

She abruptly cut off as the tip of a blade peeked through her chest. Emma's eyes widened as blood rolled down Grandmother Rel's chin and plopped onto the floor. The blade disappeared and a second later there was a loud squelching sound that could only mean one thing: the blade had been removed.

Grandmother Rel's eyes glowed gold as she worked at healing herself. Her flesh knit back together and the hole in her chest regrew. Emma had never seen someone heal so quickly before.

Grandmother Rel turned on Iris, who stood behind her. Iris' shoulders quivered and Emma wanted nothing more than to envelop her sister in a bear hug.

Grandmother Rel lifted her hand and a sword materialized within it.

As if in slow motion, Emma saw Grandmother Rel drop her arm to cut Iris down. She shot her remaining two arrows in quick succession. They puckered from Grandmother Rel's shoulder.

Grandmother Rel dropped the sword with a loud thud.

Despite the pain in her head, Emma leapt to her feet, drawing the onyx blade. Pressing down with her feet, she jumped into the air and landed on Grandmother Rel's shoulders.

With a scream of rage, Emma plunged the dagger straight into her eye.

Chapter Twenty-Five

Iris

Iris woke from the dreamworld to find Myrella engaged in a fight with Emma. Her mind took a moment to process that her sister was there. That she could come back for her.

She watched as Myrella flung Emma across the room. There was a sickening crunch as she slammed into the wall.

"The cockatrice was supposed to kill you," Myrella was saying.

Iris crawled across the floor and placed her hands on the skeleton's feet. She concentrated on breaking whatever spell animated him. She focused on snapping the bonds it had to

Myrella. The link severed with ease. She almost sensed it breathe a sigh of relief as it collapsed to the ground.

Gripping the skeleton's sword, she charged at Myrella just as she was calling Emma pathetic. With both hands, Iris raised the sword and plunged it into the witch's back. She yanked backwards, readying herself for Myrella vengeance. Myrella had just turned when Emma suddenly leapt onto the witch's head and slammed a small, black dagger into her eye.

The witch thrashed wildly as Emma ripped the blade free and leaned down to shove it into the back of her neck. Blood sprayed across the room as she nicked an artery.

Iris dropped the sword. It clattered against the stone floor as she slowly backed away. Emma leapt from Myrella's shoulders and landed on her feet as Myrella continued to shake violently. She rushed to Iris's side and took her hand.

"Are you alright?" she whispered as they watched Myrella fade into the wrinkled, spotted hag that she always had been.

Iris didn't respond. She didn't know if she could respond. She'd just helped kill the woman who raised her. Sure, she'd imagined killing Myrella over the months since she'd left them to die in the ravine. Since she'd taken Liam from her. But now that it had finally happened, she didn't know how to feel.

She glanced down at the blade still clutched in Emma's hand, a wave of recognition washing over her.

"You promised you would never use that thing," she mumured. She tugged her hand out of Emma's and took a step back. "It is an instrument of Darkness, Emmaleigh!"

Emma looked from the blade to Iris, her lips curling downwards.

"I had no other choice," she said.

There was so much sadness in her voice that Iris wanted to believe her. A part of her did. But, a larger, stronger part heard the words Rhys whispered to her as she drifted back to the real world: only trust yourself.

"You made it so that her soul has no place to go," Iris whispered. "She'll be a lost spirit."

"Serves her right," Emma spat. She turned her back on Iris.

Iris blinked at her. "How can you say that? I know she wasn't always the best guardian, but she was ours."

"You're still defending her?" Emma asked incredulously. "After all she's done to you? After she tried to kill us? Do you have any idea what I heard her say while you were still in your dream?" She crossed her arms over her chest. "Grandmother Rel promised someone—I'm not sure who—that once you convinced someone named Rhymaldis to come to her that she was going to kill you. Murder you in cold blood."

"That's not true!" Iris shouted. All the conflicting emotions she was having about Grandmother Rel's death and her role in it came flooding into her in rapid succession. She took a rattling breath. "I don't know what true or not," she whispered.

Her hands shook as she stepped towards Grandmother Rel and peered down at her. Blood covered her face and chest from the puncture wounds. She looked old. And weak. And alone.

She opened her mouth to say a prayer over Grandmother Rel's body.

A deep rumbling shook the cavern walls. Startled, she shared a glance with Emma.

"What's happening?" they asked at the exact same time.

Rocks fell from the ceiling, smashing onto the floor all around them.

"We can't stay here," Emma shouted over the wreckage.

"We have to find Liam!" Iris said. "He's here. Please, Emma, you have to help me find him."

Emma nodded. She closed her eyes for a moment.

It was agony for Iris as she watched the ceiling crumble. They would be buried in this cave if they didn't leave soon.

The temperature increased. Sweat ran in rivers down her brow. She wiped the back of her sleeve across her forehead. She panted as breathing became laborious.

Blue light streamed from Emma's chest, leading them from the room. Emma opened her eyes and started forward. Iris followed behind quickly. She felt lightheaded as the temperature in the cave continued to rise.

"I don't understand what's happening," she said.

Emma didn't respond. She began running as the cave shuddered and more rocks fell from the ceiling.

The light disappeared beyond a door at the end of a long hallway. Iris dashed ahead of Emma and twisted the doorknob. It rattled but didn't turn.

"It's locked!" she yelled as she slammed her shoulder into the door. She bounced backwards, her arm screeching in pain.

Emma pulled a long, thin dagger from her belt and jammed the tip of the blade into the locking mechanism. She twisted it this way and that for a few moments before pulling back and twisting the knob. The door swung open to reveal a small, cramped room. Liam lay on the floor, his leg trapped beneath a rock.

Iris screamed and rushed towards him. She fell to her knees and wrapped her arms around him.

"I knew you'd come," he whispered.

"Of course I came," Iris replied. Tears streamed down her cheeks as she trailed her fingers over his face, his hair, his shoulders, his torso. She needed to make sure he was really there. That they weren't locked in a dreamworld somewhere.

But he was there. He was alive.

Emma slid in beside Iris, accidently jostling the rock crushing his leg. Liam sucked in a breath, cringing.

Iris glared at her sister.

"Be careful," she hissed as she began sifting through the various bottles of potions and herbs in her satchel. She retrieved a numbing potion and carefully measured out the correct quantity into a drinking glass.

"Drink all of this," she commanded as she handed the cup to Liam.

He scowled at the vibrant green contents.

"We don't have time to argue." She pulled out lengths of cloth, then turned towards Emma and said, "We need to get that rock off him and bandage his leg as quickly as possible. The moment we remove the rock, he'll lose a lot of blood."

Emma nodded, and they both placed their hands beneath the boulder.

"On the count of three," Emma said.

"One. Two. Three," Iris said slowly.

They lifted the rock and rolled it to the side. Iris immediately shifted her attention back to Liam's crushed leg and began wrapping the worst of fractures with the linen.

Liam couldn't take the pain anymore and bit down on his own arm to stop himself from crying. He grew increasingly pale.

"You're going to be okay," Iris cooed.

She rubbed an herbal poultice into the wound and recited a short prayer to the Light for healing before finishing the wrapping.

Liam shuddered a breath and passed out.

"Help me get him out of here!" Iris shrieked as another rock dropped from the ceiling.

Something rumbled from below. Iris shared another glance with Emma as they both placed one of Liam's arms around their necks and lifted him up.

They didn't say anything as they fled the room. They moved slowly under Liam's weight. He didn't rouse as they drug him up the stairs.

Iris's legs trembled the higher they climbed. Although the air became cooler with each step they took, there was something about the way the mountain continued to shake that filled her with dread.

A roar filled the cave.

Emma yelped, startling Iris.

"What was that?" she asked.

"I don't know, but we shouldn't wait to find out," Emma replied as she crouched low and pulled Liam over her shoulder. She legs quivered as she stood.

"Are you sure you can carry him?" Iris asked. She didn't want to doubt her sister, but she also didn't want Liam to fall down several flights of stairs.

"I've got him," Emma replied. "Keep going."

She nudged Iris with her free shoulder.

Iris knew her sister was right. Whatever was down there was clearly infuriated that it had been disturbed. And now, they had no choice but to leave as quickly as possible.

Flames streamed up the stairs. Iris slammed her hand down on Emma's back, knocking all three of them to floor as a blast of fire blazed above them. Iris clutched Emma's hand.

"If we die here, I'm sorry I ever asked you to leave," she whispered. "I love you."

"I should've stayed with you, even though I angry," Emma responded.

"I'm sorry," they said at the same time and then laughed, despite the inferno right about their heads.

The stream of fire ceased a moment later. They both sprang to their feet. Iris helped Emma load Liam onto her back. They raced upwards as quickly as they could. Iris was terrified another blast of fire would kill them before they reached the cavemouth.

Before they reached safety.

She glanced behind them and her heart skipped several beats.

There, with its maw wide open and flames writhing past its teeth, was a dragon.

Chapter Twenty-Six

Emma

Emma felt her energy draining the further she carried Liam up the flight of stairs leading to their safety. He was heavy and bulky, and she was already exhausted from her journey here. Her legs wobbled as she took another step and nearly fell.

Iris's scream ripped through her. She spun around in time to see a dragon snap its mouth shut and slither up the stairs. It was bigger than the golems had been. And its eyes were intelligent as it licked its mouth.

"Run," she whispered, nudging Iris in the back. "Don't stop running."

"But—" Iris began.

"No *buts*," she replied firmly. She took another glance behind them.

I am a huntress, she reminded herself.

She met Iris's eyes. "I can't be worried about your safety," she said. She slid Liam from her shoulders. "Take him with you, if you can. If he slows you down too much, leave him."

She turned her back on her sister as she faced the dragon. She wished she had something more than her daggers and the onyx blade to fight with. She couldn't even use the bow since she'd run out of arrows.

She squared her shoulders. If she died here, she refused to let it be in vain. At the very least, she could give her sister enough time to escape. If Iris survived, it would be worth it.

Bending down, she picked up a rock, aimed, and launched it at the dragon's head. It roared with what she took to be irritation as it swung its head towards her and snarled.

"Hey, you!" she shouted. "I'm not afraid of you!"

The dragon reared up, its body swelling as it filled the hollowness of the cave. More rocks fell from the ceiling, landing all around her. She dodged being crushed by one by mere inches as she slammed her back against the wall. She drew her daggers and waited for the dragon to come closer.

While she still had the advantage of the higher ground, she leapt downwards and rammed the daggers into the dragon's snout. It hissed, licks of flame scorching her as it shook its head. She managed to rip one of the daggers out, but the other one she lost as she tumbled to the ground in a heap.

It took a step backwards and peered down at her. Its green eyes were full of sadness and confusion. Emma almost laughed at how absurd the situation was. Here she was, battling a fire-breathing dragon with no one to help her and all she could think about was how sad the dragon looked. Its black scales sparkled like rainbows as they caught the torchlight. If it hadn't been trying to kill her, she might have thought it was beautiful.

She rolled across the steps, landing in a crouching position, and darted up the stairs. The dragon snapped at her heels. She was surprised it didn't engulf her in flames. Sure, it had released puffs of flame when she'd attacked it, but it hadn't attempted to kill her directly.

She lifted the onyx dagger. She could kill it. The dagger had the ability to rip away the beast's life essence. Iris thought that meant that it destroyed souls in the name of Darkness. Maybe she was right, but there was a part of Emma who wanted to desperately believe that the dagger did more than just kill things.

She wanted to believe that it set them free.

The dragon's gaze narrowed on the dagger. She flipped it in her hand, and it trailed it with its eyes.

"Are you afraid of a little dagger?" she asked, tossing the onyx blade from one hand to the other.

The dragon crept backwards by a step. Emma raised an eyebrow. This was unexpected. She pointed the dagger at it, and it retreated a few more steps.

"How do you know to be afraid of this blade?" she mused. She approached it, still holding the dagger out before her. The dragon weaved its head from side to side, watching her warily.

She sighed heavily. She didn't want to kill the dragon if she didn't have to, but she also didn't want to leave it alive to come after her later. She'd read once that dragons enjoyed toying with their prey.

She sighed. Huntresses killed. They ignored their prey's fears. They worked alone.

She inhaled deeply. If she was going to save Iris, this was what she needed to do.

She charged forward, the dagger held in front of her. The dragon cried out, a note of fear laced with anger as it tried to retreat further down the stairs.

She leapt at it again. It batted her with a massive paw. She attempted to prick it with the dagger, but missed. Her body was flung through the air. She slammed into a wall. The wind puffed from her chest as she sank to the ground. Glass shattered, sending particles of dust and shards across the room. She waited for a moment, her lungs refilling with hot, oppressive air. When she stood, more of the sparkling dust Eldridge had given her spilled from her pant pocket.

It swirled around her. Dust particles glowed in an array of color as it floated before her face. She watched them dance on invisible waves as they twirled upwards and floated all around the dragon's head. The dragon made a loud, booming noise that reminded Emma of a sneeze before curling its tail around its legs and hunkering away.

Emma cocked her head at the dragon. It didn't seem to want to hurt her at all. If anything, it seemed like it just wanted her to leave. She laid the dagger on the ground between them and held up her hands, palms forward.

She took a step towards it. It growled and hissed, but didn't roast her, so that was a plus.

Trusting her gut instinct, she sheathed her dagger.

"See," she whispered. "I'm not going to hurt you." She held out one hand and placed it gently on the dragon's snout. For a moment, its green eyes grew wide and it stilled. It was as if it expected her to harm it. She pressed a little more firmly and said, "It's alright."

Eventually, the dragon leaned into her palm and closed its eyes.

Emma released a breath of surprise.

A smile curled the corners of her lips upwards.

"You're not trying to hurt us, are you?" she whispered. She leaned down and nuzzled the dragon. A low rumble filled the cave around them.

She didn't know dragons could purr.

"I'm sorry I attacked you," she whispered. "I don't know if you can understand me or not, but I'm not going to hurt you again." She pet the dragon's snout and smiled. "I promise."

After a moment, she remembered that Iris was somewhere nearby, struggling with Liam's limp body and terrified they were about to be eaten. She straightened, and with a sigh, continued her climb to the cavemouth.

When she looked back, all she could see were the sparkling dust particles still lingering around the dragon's head. She wondered if the dust had tamed the dragon. Eldridge had told her that it would help her seek the Light even the darkest of places. She hadn't understood it then, but maybe he'd meant that even those who seemed as if they belonged to the Darkness could be redeemed. The thought left her feeling hopeful for the future.

Sometimes violence wasn't always the right answer. Sometimes, love and patience were. The smile on her face lingered even after she caught up with Iris and Liam. They linked hands as they supported Liam between them. Together, they climbed the stairs to their freedom.

The end.

The Valka Chronicles continue in Dreamwalker

More Books by S.A. McClure

The Valka Chronicles

Spellbreaker

Starseeker

Dreamwalker (coming soon)

Broken Prophecies Series

Kilian: A Broken Prophecies Story

Keepers of the Light

Destroyers of the Light

Harbinger of the Light (coming soon)

Apprentice's Wings

Wings of Gold & Snow

Wings of Shadow & Wrath (coming soon)

Wings of Steel & Valor (coming soon)

Fortuna Saga

Spade

Suicide King (coming soon)

Dead Man's Hand (coming soon)

All or Nothing (coming soon)

About the Author

S.A. McClure is an avid lover of all things fantasy and science-fiction. A self-proclaimed nerd, S.A. enjoys attending comic cons, seeing new movies, and discussing books with friends. By day, she spends her time working with college students and by night she writes. When S.A. McClure isn't traveling, she's at home, wrangling her three trouble-making cats.

Read More from S.A. McClure

https://www.samcclure.com/

Connect with S.A. McClure

Instagram: sa_mcclure

Twitter: sa_mcclure

Facebook: SAMcClureLunameed

www.ingramcontent.com/pod-product-compliance
Lightning Source LLC
Chambersburg PA
CBHW072050170626
46813CB00004B/1281